WICKED HEARTS

BOOK FIVE IN THE SAVAGE HEARTS SERIES

MARY E. TWOMEY

MARY E. TWOMEY, LLC

WICKED HEARTS

Book Five in the Savage Hearts Series

By

Mary E. Twomey

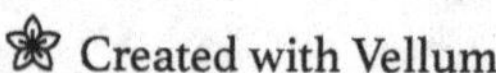 Created with Vellum

DEDICATION

For K, M and C

ABOUT WICKED HEARTS

Allies can be found in the most unexpected places.

Adelita wasn't sure what to expect when her sister came back from battling with their wicked father. A swift disbanding of the Kalku isn't as easy as everyone hoped, but every day, Adelita is determined no one else will be abducted for their evil purposes.

As an old community turns into a new ally, no one knows who to trust when things are not as they seem. Just when Adelita is sure life can't get any worse, a twist of old magic comes back to haunt Adelita in ways she never imagined.

Facing foes they have always feared is just the start of
this fast-paced conclusion to the long-awaited *Savage
Hearts* series.

1
___

HALF A MONSTER
SANTOS

Our feet drag across the sand that seems never-ending. Since traversing the sea to get to Máximo's island, we're still shaken from our encounter with the Massacooramaan. What's sticking in my mind isn't the sea monster's sharpened teeth that climbed up to his nose, or the fact that his entire body was covered in inches-long shaggy hair, nor the sight of him at probably around fifteen feet tall. What's haunting me is the fear I saw in Rafael's eyes. He wasn't afraid *for* me, he was afraid *of* me. I'm sure of it. I have lived with him long enough to know the difference. They all resisted my fighting style in the beginning, and for the most part, I've learned to adapt to their militaristic ways. Cruz, Rafi and I have mostly met in the middle—a little savagery married with a brush of calculated force. But when my death would mean my twin brother would remain imprisoned and Adelita would be without my protection, the savage in me came out.

Maybe it was too much to plunge my dagger into the ocular cavities of the Massacooramaan.

I'm still not sure I regret it. Two more soldiers are dead now, because I couldn't reach the Massacooramaan sooner and end him before he destroyed our boat.

None of us have mentioned that even after we destroy the Luz Mala (the source of Máximo's longevity and power), and free the prisoners, we have no way of getting home. We floated the rest of the way here on the remnants of our boat.

We're just as stuck here now as the slaves we came to liberate.

But that's not the thing to dwell on. One massive problem at a time.

Tavita insisted the best plan is to get to the Luz Mala, because if we fail at rescuing Santiago, at least we will have destroyed Máximo's chances at living forever.

I guess it's solid logic, but I'm a storm of restlessness inside. All I want is to find my brother and go home to Adelita.

Adelita.

I've known she was La Ciguapa from the beginning. No one could have enchanted me so quickly and permanently with the simplicity of a small smile. Having it confirmed by Tavita hasn't changed anything for me. It's being separated from her for this long that sends a dagger of pain through my side. Every step away from *mi Corazón* has been a difficult choice, but I've made it nonetheless.

I understand the balance that must be struck when you've been sucked in by La Ciguapa. Adelita could ask me for anything—even my own soul—and I would give it. The fact that I can leave her to find my twin brother is proof that Adelita will not ask me to be less than I am. My heart is more important to her than any desire to force me to tend to her whims. She knows this is the quest I must take, even though it tortures us both to be separated like this.

It's another reason why I want this job finished as quickly as possible. I need to get home to her. There's a gnawing ache in my gut, like a critter is trying to scrape away at my stomach lining until I get back to her arms. I still can't believe it's me she welcomes into her bed every night, that I am the one who gets to hold her when she is overwhelmed. I am the luckiest of all men because she runs her fingers through my hair. When I can't make sense of the world, she is kind and patient.

My bones feel wrong, moving further away from Adelita, but my soul cannot tolerate being separated from Santiago a minute longer than necessary. I'd thought him dead, ignoring the pull that told me I needed to find him. I saw him get stabbed by one of the elders in the cave the day I was liberated.

We were both supposed to die that day.

It's the practice of the Kalku to kill off the slaves if the cave is compromised, but Cruz and the others got to me before the deadly blow could be dealt. I was cursed with muteness, so any mourning I felt at my twin's supposed passing was silenced.

It's the habit of Cáceres to kill off the Kalku and free the cave slaves. They take us back to the person's previous home or to a hospital and leave them to what they hope is a better life.

But I'd had no previous home, since I had been with the Kalku since I was a baby. I am fortunate Cruz and Rafael took me to Cáceres. Their love kept me alive. Kept me sane.

They gave me a new family on the day I lost my brother.

It's what should have happened to both Santiago and me, but only I lived through the raid.

Santiago, had been killed off, or so I thought. But Tavita informed us that my twin brother was taken to Máximo's island to do the evil maniac's bidding.

"I need to stop," Rafael admits, though I know he is

speaking up for Tio Bruno's sake. No one is bold enough to tell the military man that he should be thinking about retiring, so Rafi takes the label of being the weakest link to give Tio Bruno a break. We've all seen better days. The fight with Massacooramaan came on the heels of the slaughter of half our militia.

Tavita's spine straightens when we stop to sit. She stands over us, like a mama bear guarding her rambunctious boys. She sniffs the air, so I follow suit. My human nose picks up the typical scents: sand, ocean, bark, foliage. But there's a note of something else that's organic and new to me. I can't quite make it out.

I shift into my wolf, stick my nose to the sand and then poise it in the air.

Animal, that's for sure. Though this one smells... off. Like dog, only stronger.

I tilt my head up at Tavita, wondering if her stiffened posture is because she smells the same thing.

When she senses my gaze is fixed on her, she bends down and runs her fingers over my fur.

Because she is Adelita's sister, I allow it.

Tavita angles her chin away from the Luz Mala—the green beam of light we have been walking toward. "You smell that, too? I was afraid this might happen. We might be too late to stop Máximo completely."

I sneeze at her.

"We might have to be quieter, moving forward. Máximo had a plan, back when I lived on the island. He liked to abduct men that the Kalku had mutated into cadejos (or shifters). Máximo would take their animal and experiment on it, changing it. I don't know how he did it, but his goal was to make their animals into monsters."

Rafi's neck shrinks as he stretches out his legs across the cool sand. The night air breezes past us, but it's Rafi's words that send a chill up my spine. "I was one of the first cadejos in the cave when I was little. Or, I was supposed to be, anyway. I was liberated before they could finish my animal."

Tavita turns to him and finally sits in the sand. "That must have been awful. Is that why you halfway shifted in the water?"

Rafi snorts. "Nah. I'm not all that sure if my animal can swim, so I was purposefully trying to keep him from coming out. But when he went after Santos, I had a hard time holding back." He fixes his eyes on the volcano that contains the Luz Mala inside. It's still a good few hours' distance away. "Adelita kissed me a while ago, and it did something to my animal. It healed him. Completed him. So I can be full-on monster now, if I want to."

Tio Bruno and Tavita gape at his confession. Tio

Bruno's nostrils flair. "It's a fine time to tell us that! I saw your snout grow, and that was news to me. I thought maybe I was seeing things, or that I didn't remember what your animal looked like. It's been a long time since you've shifted in front of me." He tilts his head skyward. "Adelita did this? She pushed your animal along, and now it's a full-blown dragon? What else do we not know about this girl?"

Rafi smirks but still watches the volcano. "I would imagine there's a great deal we don't know about her. Cruz, Santos and I know more because we took the time to earn her trust. And honestly, she didn't know she could heal people with her kisses, much less complete my transition."

Tio Bruno's volume rises. "What?"

Rafi grimaces. "Did I not mention that? It's how she was able to heal my dragon. She kissed me, and her mojo did its thing. But she kissed Santos' face before that. That's the *real* story behind his scars smoothing out."

Tio Bruno frowns and stares at me, even though I'm in my wolf form. "So I guess the story you fed us before about finding a special cream was a giant lie."

Rafi holds the flat of his hand parallel to the ground and tilts it from side to side. "Would we call that a giant lie?"

Tio Bruno rolls his eyes and then addresses me. "So Adelita kissed your cheek, and your scars healed?"

I bob my head.

Rafi claps his own shoulder. "She healed up a gash from a knife fight, too."

Tavita bites down on her lower lip, stepping back. Her limp has always been there, but it's worse after all we have been through to get to the island. "This is bad. I thought I understood why Máximo wants Adelita so badly. Sure, he wants his curse lifted, and she could make that happen. But she can also complete a cadejo's transition. If a shifter's animal has been badly mutated, she could heal them. Complete them. That's nearly every slave on this island. Máximo wants an army of cadejos, so he takes ones the Kalku have already made. Then he mutates their animal to make it more deadly. If Adelita can kiss one of them that's half-mutated and complete their transition?" She shakes her head. "I don't want to know how lethal Máximo could become."

Rafi shakes his head. "My dragon isn't more deadly. It's complete now. I'm able to fully shift."

"Making it more deadly," she finishes.

Rafi ducks his chin. "Oh. I guess you're right. But my animal isn't crazy or anything. My dragon would never take orders from Máximo."

Tavita touches the spot behind her ear where

Máximo had implanted a listening device. We had it removed, but I know it haunts her. "You don't know that. If Máximo wants something, he takes it. Father sacrificed someone so he could control my actions and override my better judgment. Who's to say he can't do the same to you, once he gets his hands on your dragon?"

I swallow hard, green light shining out of the volcano.

Tio Bruno's hand finds Tavita's back. Now that it's only Rafi and me as his audience, he doesn't hold back his attachment to her as much. "What are we up against? What sort of animal is Máximo making?"

Tavita swallows hard. "You'll know it when you see it. The animal is nothing like I have ever witnessed in nature. They are not themselves when they shift. In their human form, they're cave slaves under Máximo's rule, but they still have their wits about them. They can still think for themselves. But in their animal form, they only do his bidding. If you see one, you're probably as good as dead."

My head jerks back and I let out a sneeze of protest. No cadejo is going to best me. I mean, honestly. Not to toot my own horn, but I just took down a sea monster in the middle of the water. Plus, I've never heard of a shifter's animal not obeying its human counterpart. That's ridiculous.

The caution in Tavita's eyes gives my bravado pause.

When we start toward the volcano again, I keep to my wolf, my nose working overtime to track down any encroaching enemies before they attack us.

Tio Bruno offers his arm to Tavita, compensating for the limp that seems to stem from her hip. He is good at being there for her, silently helping her without bringing attention to his kindness or her shortcomings.

I like them together. Tio Bruno is insufferable apart from her.

I need to find to Santiago. I need to get him out of here.

No matter who I have to take down, I will bring my brother home.

2

TAVITA'S PLAN
RAFAEL

I have no idea if we are being followed. Santos and Tavita seem to be more attuned to that sort of thing. But since they keep moving us forward and nothing has jumped out to attack us, I guess onward we go.

The closer we get to the volcano, the rockier the terrain grows. The sand deserted us a while ago, and now our damp clothing stretches uncomfortably as we try not to trip and scrape ourselves up on the black boulders.

"It's as if Máximo doesn't want us to find the Luz Mala," I complain when Tavita's narrower foot gets lodged between two rocks. Tio Bruno wiggles the limb loose, but it's slow going, for sure. That, and we're out in the open without a stitch of foliage anywhere around to conceal us. We have only the moonlight for cover, and soon enough, even that will be gone.

The nearer we get to the volcano, though, the more we are aware of every snap of twig and rustle of wind.

When I get anxious, I can't turn off my mouth. Cruz usually just ignores me and lets me talk until I'm blue in the face. I can tell Tio Bruno wants me to shut up, but I can't stop myself. "I used to hear stories about people trying to go over to the island to kill Máximo, but those tales stopped a long time ago. I think most people are more concerned with the Kalku than they are with him. Everyone assumes that because he's on his island, he's not an immediate danger to us."

Tavita lets out a derisive puff of air. "No one on the mainland knew there were slaves over here. They have no idea what Máximo is planning. It's a pure case of ignorance being bliss. I was stuck over here for two years. Only one group of soldiers made it over, and it was because Máximo wanted me taken back to the mainland, so I could bring Adelita to him. He practically giftwrapped me for them."

"I didn't know," Tio Bruno confesses, his hand on the small of her back as we move forward. His voice is strained with the pain of her agony. It's the same twisted-gut sound Santos gets when Adelita is upset. "If I had known you were here, I would have come for you."

Tavita casts him a sliver of her smile. "You didn't know me back then, but thanks all the same."

The air is dense here. I can feel it affecting my limbs, weighting them beyond my normal springy step. Though the volcano looks dormant enough, not giving off noticeable heat, I'm sweating from the different climate on the island.

Or maybe the sweat is evidence of pure terror. I'm not sure.

When we finally reach the foot of the volcano, Tavita shakes out her hands, as if gearing herself up.

"What's the plan? You said you could get the Luz Mala out of the volcano. Is there a rope or something around here for us to climb up and lower ourselves down?"

Tavita keeps her eyes from us, blowing out a long breath. "Nothing quite so obvious. I'll take it from here."

I quirk my brow at her. "And what exactly does that entail?"

She motions to the immovable rock wall before us. "I'm going to walk through the side."

I purse my lips. "Come again?"

Tavita speaks to me as if I'm slow. "I can walk through walls. This is a wall. I'm going to walk through it and grab the Luz Mala inside."

I fight with my exasperation. "That's your big idea?

This isn't a regular wall with studs and whatnot. This is thick rock, Tavita." I glance at Tio Bruno. "Did you know this was her plan?"

Tio Bruno nods once. I can tell he is not thrilled about it either.

Tavita waves off my concern, but I can tell from the quaver in her voice that she is scared. "This is easy. I used to walk through walls all the time. Just because I haven't gone through a volcano before doesn't mean anything. This is nothing."

Tio Bruno postures, his hand rubbing slowly across her back to soothe her nerves. "How can I be helpful, Blue Eyes?"

I blanch at their cuteness. I am no one to begrudge a couple their gag-worthy moments, but listening to Tio Bruno say anything sweet is beyond strange.

"Just keep the coast clear out here. Máximo said it was a gold cup filled with emeralds. Shouldn't be too hard to find in there." She points to the green light floating over the volcano. "But when I pick it up and the light moves, I'm not sure how we'll be able to keep a low profile."

She places both her hands onto the volcano wall, leaning forward and putting her weight onto her palms. It's like she is expecting to fall through. "Gotta soften the barrier first," she explains. "You don't just walk right through something." She says it like we all know how obvious that is.

When nothing happens, she pulls back and shakes out her hands again. "The walls are thicker here. Could you all stop staring? I'm on the edge of frustration already. If I can't get through this, then we came all this way for nothing."

I raise my hand. "I could try climbing up the volcano."

"And jumping into the bottom of the abyss?" Tavita shakes her head. "Just give me some time. If I don't do this properly, I'll get stuck between the walls."

Tio Bruno goes on high alert. "Wait, what? That's possible? I don't like it. We'll do the other thing—climbing up the side and jumping into the hole."

"That's suicide. You can't act rashly, Beautiful. Give me a minute and I'll get through just fine."

These two with the sweetheart names. Gross. I've never heard anyone describe the surly military commander as beautiful.

Tio Bruno's eyes close. "I will tear this volcano apart with my bare hands if you get caught inside the walls."

Tavita replies with a cool, "I'm counting on it. Now shush and go stand over there. Your tight butt is distracting me. If you keep staring, I'll have no choice but to strip you naked and ride you right here in front of the guys. I don't think that's something they will enjoy."

Tio Bruno smiles and, if I'm seeing correctly, he's blushing? Well, that's downright cute.

And also gross.

Tavita waits until Tio Bruno takes a few steps back before she presses her arms to the walls and closes her eyes. I probably shouldn't be staring, but I can't help it. I have never seen anyone walk through a wall before.

Santos sniffs the rock, his tail wagging as he catches different scents. I'm never sure what his wolf does with that information, but it seems important to him.

It is several long minutes before Tavita steps back, shaking out her hands and bending her knees, like she's getting ready for a race. "That should do it, I hope."

"How will we know if it works?"

Tavita stretches her arms over her head. "Well, you'll either see me in a few minutes or you'll never see me again." She speaks as if her voice carries a shrug, but when the words hit the air, she shudders. "Look after Adelita, alright?" She's not looking at me or Santos. She knows the four of us take care of each other. Instead, her eyes fix on Tio Bruno. "Promise me."

Tio Bruno swallows hard. "I promise. You'll come back to me, though. Then we'll look after her together.

Though I cannot imagine she could possibly get into more trouble than she's already done."

"She needs family. She's been alone for too long."

If she thinks Tio Bruno is the type to be all warm and welcoming, I seriously question her judgment.

Tio Bruno holds his hand over his heart. "Whatever Adelita needs, I'll see to it. On my honor."

She moves to stand in front of him. "Then I know it'll get done. Thank you." Though she's nearly six feet tall, Tio Bruno still has her beat by a few inches, so she leans up on her toes to kiss him once more before moving back to the volcano's edge.

"More," Tio Bruno begs. "Soften the barrier some more. I don't want you to risk getting stuck."

"Can't. If I soften it more than this, the whole thing might crumble. Then we'll have a real mess on our hands."

Her steadying breath does nothing to calm my worries. Even as she takes a step, her leg vanishing, I can't enjoy the wonder of it all. I'm too anxious that we might actually lose her. With her goes the only hope of getting the Luz Mala out of the volcano. If we are going to take out Máximo, we'll have to destroy his immortality first.

When Tavita's whole body disappears, Tio Bruno hangs his head. "What did we just do?"

Santos sits at his feet in a move of solidarity. He understands what it is to be connected to La Ciguapa, and the pain it takes to see them walk into a danger you cannot stop.

The three of us wait in silence, until the still of the night is broken by the baritone bray of an animal I cannot quantify.

Santos is on high alert, the upper lip of his maw curling to let me know someone unwelcome is approaching.

The hairs on the back of my neck stand up as I turn toward the rest of the island, hoping we haven't bitten off more than we can chew.

3

___

A MONSTER NAMED JAIME

SANTOS

I am not Tio Bruno's biggest fan, but I feel a kinship with him. Being tied to La Ciguapa women as we are means I am one of two people who understand his angst right now. As my eyes comb the horizon for movement, I stay close to his heels, making sure that when Tavita comes back from fetching the Luz Mala from inside the dormant volcano, no harm will have befallen her mate.

"She limps," Tio Bruno says quietly to me in a mournful tone. "Máximo hurt her. Over and over he tortured Tavita. The fact that he's here on this island? I want to tear him apart. I need him dead."

I lower my head, communicating that it will be done. Máximo is sick to hurt his own flesh and blood.

The animal's low call wouldn't pull my focus at all,

but for Tavita's warning that on this island there are shifters who were taken by Máximo so he could experiment with their animal. I am not sure how deadly a mutated cadejo here might be, but I am not willing to risk Tio Bruno's safety, or Rafi's, for that matter.

I hedge the both of them in, herding them to stand with their backs to the volcano. If anyone is going out there to investigate, it'll be me. I am one of them, after all—a cadejo. I can only hope the enslaved shifters understand that and back off accordingly.

Was Santiago experimented on? Was he taken and tortured? What is his animal now? We were identical wolves, way back when we were cave slaves for the Kalku. My wolf is much the same, except the scarring is gone. I can only hope my brother is out there, still himself in some way.

When the foreign animal's call comes nearer, I snort at Rafi, letting him know I will handle this. We have been together long enough that he knows my verbal, nonverbal and wolfish cues.

My paws are careful on the jagged black rocks. It's not dawn yet, but the light from the Luz Mala shining up from the center of the volcano sheds enough illumination for my wolf's eyes to pick out the details in the distance.

I trot out to meet the shape, but as I near, the animal

paws at the sand, saying something either to me or to his buddies that I cannot decipher. With a twist of magic, I slip out of my wolf and rise up onto two legs. "Santiago. I need to see Santiago. I am his twin brother, come to collect him and take him home."

As I walk nearer, the shadows give way to a shape I can barely make sense of. He is on four legs—that much I can tell. But he's hairless with gray skin stretched taut over bulging ribs. His nose is long, and on his head there is a spiked fin that stretches all the way down his back to a tail that flicks curiously.

Is that a cat's tail?

I don't understand what I'm looking at.

Is he a dog? A shark? A lizard?

I see that the animal is far larger and longer than an average dog. He's more like a mid-sized horse with a spiny shark fin or something on his back. He brays, and it feels like a warning, like he's trying to tell me something, but I cannot guess what.

His clawed front legs press hard on the sand, bowing his front half, breathing hard like he's in pain. His neck stretches out, and his head turns into that of a human. "Go!" he pleads. "I don't know how you got here, but if you don't get out now, you'll die on this island! Go, before he finds you!"

My chest puffs. "I am not afraid of Máximo. Santiago

needs me. I am not leaving without him. Can you tell me where he is?"

The cadejo is mid-transition and looks like he is in some serious pain. "Máximo sometimes has more control over our animals than we do! I can't get out of my animal all the way anymore! I'm trying, but I can't! Help me! If I don't shift into a person, I'll bite your throat and suck out your blood! Run!"

I take a step forward, though that might be a foolish move. "I don't know what it is to be afraid of your animal. I won't leave you like this. Lie down and close your eyes."

The man obeys with a whine of distress. "My animal was a panther before this. Now my tail is all that's left of him. I don't always know what my monster is going to do. Please, sir. Put me down! Kill me before I kill one of the others!"

I kneel beside him, stroking my hand over his head and down his smooth, hairless back. "I have no desire to end your life. You can get control of this thing. We all had to struggle at first. Remember when you first met your panther? You had to remind him who ran the show."

"This is different. My monster wants to please Máximo, not me. You have to run!"

I wince at the admission. "We can't very well fight

you all, can we. I don't want to hurt a fellow shifter whose animal doesn't belong to him. Think hard. Who were you? Tell me about the man, not the monster."

"Jaime," he breathes. "My name is Jaime. I have a wife and three children. I was liberated from the Kalku when I was seven, but I was stolen again... I'm not sure when. It's hard to keep track of time here. Take me back to them." Then his eyes widen and he shakes his head in a frantic rhythm. "But don't let me near them! I don't want to murder my family. I can't... I can't do this! Help me!"

"Jaime," I coo. "That's good. Hold on to yourself. Hold your wife's face in your heart." But even as I say the words, I can feel his struggle. "Help me find Santiago. Where is he?"

He paws at the sand, his hands a mixture of fingers and claws. "Back at the palace."

"There's a palace in this place?"

The man has the wherewithal to snort. "That's what Máximo calls his house. Santiago soothes Máximo with a song when he cannot sleep, so Santiago usually sleeps on the sand outside the palace."

My mind blanches that my brother doesn't have a bed.

Santiago can have mine. It's done. It's decided. I sleep in Cruz's room now, anyway.

I fight to keep my focus. "Tell me where there's a boat. Ours was destroyed by the Massacooramaan on the way over here."

Jaime shakes his head. "My monster doesn't want me to tell you. He's already mad at me! He's going to make me suffer."

"How does he hurt you?" This is so messed up. To have your animal changed into something else is one thing, but to not have control over that beast is unthinkable. I cannot imagine the struggle that must come for these slaves daily.

This was an experiment gone horribly wrong.

"He'll chew the skin off my arms or run me headfirst into a wall over and over." Jaime's breathing syncopates, letting me know that each sentence costs him a great deal of effort. "Chupacabra," he says with a mourning lilt. "That's what Máximo calls our monsters. We drink the blood of animals. Some days, that's all he will let us eat. Máximo is grooming us to lose our humanity, craving the taste of blood so much that there will be no desire to transition back onto two legs."

I gape at him, unable to offer anything comforting. Máximo is the monster, of that much, I am certain. Jaime's Chupacabra needs healing. It needs...

A light of hope shines in my brain. "If you can help me with this, I can take you to someone who might be able to heal your animal. I've seen it happen." It's an overpromise, though not outside the realm of possibility. "But first we have to get Santiago and a boat. If there are others who need rescuing, give me a list of names. Otherwise, they stay here with Máximo."

The man opens his mouth, but a garbled bray tumbles out, spooking me enough to teeter back on my heels. His claws have hard, sharp edges that look just as deadly as his jagged teeth.

I can see why Tavita was frightened of them.

"The boats are on the shore near the palace! That way," Jaime says, jerking his head over his shoulder. "Go! Go now!"

"We can't. We have a job to finish up here first. Deep breaths. Your animal is not stronger than you." I say it with confidence, but truthfully, I have no idea what I'm talking about. This man looks like he's in some real pain. I run my hand over his hair again, soothing his angst as best I can.

A feral snarl rips from the man's lips, chilling my spine.

It's then I see him losing the fight with his Chupacabra. His head begins to mutate, his maw elongating and his teeth turning to weapons sharp enough to shred flesh with a single swipe.

I frantically try to figure a way to best him without

wounding the man, and finally land on a forceful blow to the top of his head.

It takes three hard hits before Jaime's animal goes limp beneath my fist. Within seconds, he is a man with no trace of animal to him. His lips are parted and his body is incapacitated.

Though I only met Jaime, sadness crests over any sense of relief from my small victory. He is a cadejo, like me, and doesn't deserve the wrath of my fist.

So this is what my life has come to.

I need to get this man to his family. But first, we have to find my brother and the boat.

That is, if Tavita ever makes it back out of the volcano. If not, I'm not sure how we'll pry Tio Bruno away from this island.

4

———

BURIED

ADELITA

orse than being found out is not knowing if the person who now has discovered one of your biggest secrets can be trusted not to exploit it. When Cruz, Eva and I traveled to Anzaldúa to ask them for a safe place to hide, we realized we would be at their mercy. What we didn't expect was to be taken below the earth's surface under the pretense of being criminals, and then locked inside of a room that was encased in packed dirt.

Eva didn't know about my unnatural strength until Salvador trapped us in the solid cement room far beneath the earth's surface. I had to break my secret to her so I could try to get us out.

Though, even my strength didn't gain us our freedom, so it was pretty anticlimactic. Apparently, this little room was Salvador's way of extracting the truth out of us faster than any torture ever could.

While I applaud his nonviolent methods, I would pummel this pleasantly smug jackass if I knew how to get out of here. But we wound down so many unlit subterranean hallways that I fear finishing off Salvador might end our only chances at ever seeing the sunshine again.

Plus, Cruz already knocked him out cold with a single punch.

Eva moves over to me to hold my hand, her body angled in front of mine. Even though we both know I should be shielding her, she is fiercely protective of her people.

That's when it dawns on me that *I* am her people. I belong somewhere.

And it's not cowering in the corner, hiding in shame that I am this odd creature nature should never have allowed.

I step out from behind her and prod Salvador with the toe of my sneaker. "Wake up, Salvador. We've got a bone to pick with you. This is no time for a nap."

It takes a few groans, but eventually, Salvador sits up, massaging his jaw. "I guess I should've seen that coming." His eyes flick to me. "I suppose I should be grateful it wasn't you who hit me." His voice is gravelly.

Even though I am furious with him, part of me wishes I had a lozenge to offer.

Cruz folds his arms over his broad chest. "Yeah? Well, that was the warmup assault. If you don't tell us what's going on right now, Adelita is coming for you next. So I'd get real chatty real quick."

"We don't believe in torture, here in Anzaldúa," Salvador explains, though this opener doesn't inspire much confidence. "But I needed to know what you were hiding. If Máximo is after you, it's important I understand why, so I know what to guard against. If you came in here with a weapon that could harm my people, I have a right to that information."

Eva stands at my side. "Sure, but you don't have the right to lock us up after promising to help."

Salvador stands, wobbling slightly on the way up. None of us offers to help steady him.

Salvador gives Eva the appropriate penitent expression, his chin tilted toward the floor. "Fair enough. Apologies all the way around. Now that I know Máximo's daughter has incredible strength, there's no need for further information extraction." He opens and closes his jaw slowly, wincing at the power packed in Cruz's punch. "Shall I take you to your rooms?"

I don't trust this guy at all, but we have no other choice. I hold onto Eva's hand, making it clear that any camaraderie he was hoping to establish has now been blown to pieces. "Lead the way."

We go back into the hallway, which is flooded with black. There's not a stitch of light when Salvador flicks off the switch in the room and leads us forward. I feel my way along the wall, holding onto Eva's hand as if it's the only thing keeping me from drowning. The dark is all-encompassing, like a creeping presence I can feel on my skin.

Though we're already who knows how far underground, the packed-dirt floor slopes yet further downward, giving me the sensation of walking straight into my own grave. This is a lot of trust to put in a man who's already tricked us once.

When that thought dawns on me, my feet come to a sudden stop. Eva tugs at my hand, but I refuse to move. "Addy, this way."

"No." At my firm refusal to walk another step, I note the absence of the other two sets of footsteps. "I'm not going any further."

"We don't have a choice. There's no way we can find a path out of here." Eva's fright is my own, but my stubborn nature is vexed just enough to rear its ugly head.

My upper lip curls. "Then I'll die in the dark. I don't trust you, Salvador. You could be leading us to another friendly little interrogation. I'm tired. I'm done with this.

We needed a safe place to hide, not to be groomed with fear and be forced to call it trust."

Cruz is silent, which means he most likely agrees with Eva that we should keep going. Part of me does, too, or I wouldn't have taken that first step. But I've hit my limit, and cannot budge another inch without good reason.

Salvador strides toward me until he's close enough that I can smell his aftershave. He whispers just loud enough for Cruz and Eva to hear, his raspy cadence muted somewhat when his volume lowers. "Do you know why we use dirt instead of concrete for the floors and walls down here?" When I don't respond, he supplies the answer. "Because concrete echoes. The dirt absorbs sound better, but not entirely. I'm fairly certain we haven't been followed, but if you want absolute anonymity down here, I suggest we get out of the open halls and into my home. Our ears are keener than yours because we're used to the sounds down here. I trust my people, but I promised to hide you, so I'm hiding you even from them. That is how deep my word goes."

Salvador touches my wrist, but I flinch away. No part of my body is his to handle. "Not good enough. I have no reason to trust any of that is true."

Salvador hesitates, and I can tell he's trying to come up with something better than his logic. "Okay, how about this. You're giving me your trust to get you to my home, and I'm giving you my signet ring to wear until we get there. You can give it back once we're safely inside my home."

Salvador picks up my free hand and slides a heavy ring onto my thumb.

"You better not have found this thing in a cereal box," I mutter, to which, Salvador chuckles.

"No," Cruz protests firmly, while still respecting the quiet tone Salvador is trying to set. "You don't put a ring on her finger. She is not yours."

Cruz's indignation has the note of a boyfriend who has been wronged.

Salvador takes the scolding in stride as he slides the ring off. "Very well. Lady Eva, will you wear my ring?"

His gravelly voice carries the note of something weighty and vulnerable. It's a strange way to phrase his question, for sure.

The tremble in Eva's reply tells me I'm not the only one who notices the shift in the air. "Are you deserving?"

I keep my grip on her other hand, but step away to afford them the illusion of privacy.

Salvador's voice lowers. That same slice of vulnerability pokes through. "Is anyone? On my honor, I will do all I can not to make you regret my ring on your finger."

Holy smokes. What did I miss? How long have they been talking prior to our visit?

"Very well," Eva says with equal amounts of insecurity and bravado. "You may indulge your fantasy for now."

Salvador snickers at Eva's moxie. Gotta love a girl who won't lower herself off the pedestal she was raised on.

Eva reaches out and rests my hand in Cruz's, I'm guessing taking Salvador's arm instead. The mood has definitely turned.

As Salvador leads the way with Eva on his arm, Cruz and I follow with silent steps. With my arm looped around the crook of Cruz's elbow, I get the sneaking sensation that I'm walking down the aisle at Eva's wedding to Salvador. There's something stately to the stiffness of my spine now. While I've never been in a wedding before, my steps are measured now, as if my body understands the importance of what's happening better than my logical brain will allow.

"Does this seem strange?" Cruz whispers to me. "Did all that sound a bit... serious?"

"Salvador is nothing if not strange. And yes. That was... That was something." I'm grateful for the heat of Cruz's body. There's a chill underground that tightens my joints.

Salvador breaks our secrets with a sing-song voice. "I can hear you, you know. My ears are far better attuned to things down here. It's only serious if Lady Eva allows. She is not unaware of my affection for her."

It's like he's admitting to wanting to marry Eva, while also making it all seem silly and off the cuff. I can't get a read on this guy. It's disarming, and I'm not sure I like it.

Cruz puts words to my confusion. "How long have you two been talking?"

Eva says, "None of your business," at the same time Salvador replies with a cool, "About a year."

Cruz hisses his opinion. "You could have at least told Dad that you'd already chosen a suitor."

"Phone calls in secret are not the same as in-person meetings. Until today, I hadn't seen Salvador or his father in a decade. I haven't chosen anything other than to be loyal to Cáceres." Her voice lowers. "Dad would never allow me to marry someone outside of Cáceres, so it's all moot anyway."

I can tell Cruz is none too pleased, but he can't very well tell Eva what to do. She's a grown woman. The sauciest thing she's done is talk on the phone.

My thumb drags over Cruz's bicep.

He flinches at my touch. "Salvador, how much farther? Adelita's fingers are freezing. She needs a sweater or gloves or something."

"Just a minute or two. Not far at all. I do apologize for my thoughtlessness. I should have brought a blanket for your Ciguapa."

I don't like when Salvador calls me that—as if I'm a weird thing or a pet, and not a person. As if the only reason Cruz could care about me so sweetly is if nefarious magic was somehow involved.

Though, perhaps that might be a bit of my own insecurities peeking out and pinning themselves on Salvador's words.

Cruz's hovering is so sweet, and not at all how I'd thought he would ever be when in a relationship. Though, upon closer inspection, this is the fighter who notices everything. He is always calculating weaknesses so his people survive. He's never at rest because he will not tolerate breaches in his security. I guess that could translate to how he treats me, as well.

I love the thoughtfulness, but I don't want him getting all tense every time my fingers get chilly. "I'm really okay," I tell them.

But Cruz is uninterested in me pacifying his worry. He drags my fingers to his lips and blows warm air on them, and then tucks my hand under his armpit. It's above and beyond considerate, and I love him for the sweetness.

True to his word, it doesn't take more than a minute

or two to reach a door. Salvador fiddles with a key, and finally, light floods the corridor.

The three of us flinch at the bright intrusion. Cruz cups the back of my head, smashing my face into his chest to protect my eyes.

My hand lands on his firm chest, stroking lightly to ease his anxiety. He may not voice his worries, but I can feel them like the restless tide lapping at his resolve to appear impassive and unshakable.

Yet as he buries his face in my hair, I realize that he trusts me with his vulnerable spots. He knows I will protect him as he does the same for me.

This is a relationship. I like this.

"Sorry," Salvador says. "I should have warned you about the light. The bulbs are barely thirty watts, but it can take some getting used to. It gets brighter as you go further in, so take your time adjusting." Then his voice lowers to a saccharine coo. "It's alright, Lady Eva. Take a few breaths."

The moment I can blink the world into focus, I turn my head, squinting at Salvador and Eva in the doorway. They have the same posture Cruz and I do—his arms around her and her face buried in his chest. It's an odd sight, to be sure, but it's nice to see Eva in the arms of someone she trusts this much.

Though, whether or not Salvador is worthy of that trust is still a matter of opinion.

Salvador catches me watching him, and offers a friendly smile accompanied by a jerk of his head. "Shall we?"

He keeps Eva's hand because it's a prize not many can win.

Once we're all inside, Salvador shuts the door and locks it. "This is my home. It's soundproof, so there's no worry anyone will hear you and find you out. Everything in here is the same as homes on the outside—running water, plumbing, ventilation, kitchen."

He guides us through an olive-painted entryway into... well, it's a normal home. Fresh out of suburbia, with the only notable difference being that the ceilings are slightly lower than I'm used to. There's precious little clutter in the kitchen he takes us through, pulling down glasses and filling them with water from the tap. He passes them around, reminding me just how thirsty I am.

Salvador taps a pad of paper magnetized to the fridge. "Anything you need, simply write it on this list and I'll see to it. Your bags are already in your rooms, though I didn't know who is sharing rooms with whom, so feel free to sleep wherever."

Cruz's stomach growls, so I speak up. "Is there anything to eat?"

Salvador smiles at me, clearly pleased I trust him enough to ask for food and assume it hasn't been poisoned. "There is. I can heat up some stew I made yesterday while you get settled."

The walls are bright white, and above us the ceiling is painted to look like a midday sky on a summer's day. It's cheery, if not whimsical and a little endearing.

Salvador leans back on the counter and then pops his body up so he can sit on his white and gold marbled countertop. "You forgive me for eavesdropping?" he asks with faux penitence in his exaggerated frown.

Eva's nose lifts. "Should I?"

Cruz's arm hasn't left my body this entire time. He eyes Salvador, still sizing him up. "Do what you have to, but the more on edge you keep me, the worse it's going to be for you once I snap. You can take whatever gamble you like on those odds."

Fair point.

"I've never seen an Acalica at work before. We don't have any of your kind in our village. Since I cuffed you, it's been raining hard. When you were trapped in the interrogation room, the rain turned to a storm. Any idea when that's going to let up?"

Cruz is unconcerned. "I guess that depends on how far you plan on pushing my temper."

"I'm done pushing. You can relax in here. No one comes in without my say-so. Feel free to wait out Máximo as long as you like."

"Will our phones work underground?"

"They will if you let me put an attachment on them."

I can tell Eva doesn't like this caveat one bit. "You're not listening in on my phone calls."

"No, I'm not. And this device won't. You don't have to use it, but if you want to touch base with the outside world, it's your only option."

Eva's shoulders slump. "One of us has to, Cruz. It should be my phone, I'm guessing. The Kalku would tap into your phone first out of all of us."

I raise my hand. "Can't tap into my phone. I don't have one."

Cruz closes his eyes. "Fine. I hate this. It's too much trust we have to give over for impossible reasons. If you were hoping to make peace with our tribe, this is a weird way to go about it."

Salvador's heels kick a light rhythm on the cupboard. "I'm hoping to help Cáceres by hiding you. Trust and peace aren't something I can control." Then he hops down off the counter. "Come, let me show you the rest of the place. You can go anywhere you like, except for this hallway just around there, which I keep locked, so that shouldn't be a problem."

Eva's eyebrow raises, and I can tell she's already trying to think up a way to get on the other side of that door. What she expects to find, I couldn't say, but I can tell she's not going to let that go any time soon.

I couldn't care less what's behind the door. It's Salvador's house, not mine. Boundaries are healthy, and I'll not begrudge him some privacy.

Salvador leads us to another stretch, nodding his head toward the rooms after he motions to the pile of our backpacks in the hallway. "I didn't know your preferred sleeping arrangements, so I have a cot set up in my office for the third bed. But this here is my guest bedroom, and this is a lounge area with a sofa that pulls out. Sorry I couldn't be more accommodating. People tend to notice if you have a new mattress brought down, and then three outsiders appear."

Cruz pokes his head into the guest room. "You okay if we take this, Eva? It's a queen. I'm not sure if Addy and I would both fit on a sofa."

Eva holds her head up, swallowing her sigh. "That's fine. I'll take the sofa, Salvador. You can put away the cot and still use your office."

"You're not accounting for the late-night movies I like to watch in the lounge area."

Eva casts him a flirty smile. "Then I guess I'll have to scoot over and make room for you."

His chest puffs at the blatant invitation. Pure hunger dances in his eyes as he takes a step toward her. Then, as if remembering that they don't know each other well enough for such things yet, he shrinks back. "I'll see to your dinner. Should be ready in twenty minutes or so."

He skirts back to the kitchen, leaving us to settle in. Cruz nods to his sister and then opens the door for me, shutting the two of us in the guest bedroom.

"Do you think we can trust him?" I ask Cruz as he sets our bags atop the white linens.

"Never." He turns his chin to the right and the left, cracking his neck. "His father is the reason our tribes don't get along. This is the first time anyone from Cáceres has reached out to them for help in at least two decades."

"What did Salvador's father do?"

Cruz's tone is grave. "There was an insurrection in Anzaldúa, so he buried half his tribe. Then he ground up their bodies and mixed them in the soil. He used the dirt to build this underground city. Some of our people were visiting and got the same treatment. Same as a dozen or so from the Mendez tribe. No one's reached out to Anzaldúa in ages. Trust runs real thin around here."

My stomach roils. "What? Are you serious?" I look down at the packed dirt. "Does that mean..."

Cruz stamps his boot down twice. "I didn't want to say anything to you, but yeah. We're standing on the burial ground of about a thousand citizens of Anzaldúa." His voice lowers. "So if you meet Don Luis, tread lightly. If we're lucky, we won't see him at all, and we'll get out of here without him finding out who we are."

"And if he does?" This is really something that should have been covered before we made this trek.

Cruz turns his back to me, unzipping his pack. "If Don Luis gets wind that the prince and princess of Cáceres are in his village, we might not make it out of here alive."

5

LUZ MALA
SANTOS

There isn't anything to bind up the cadejo, so I leave him in the grass and run back to the volcano, hoping Tavita has returned. It's bad enough that she could be in actual danger in there, stuck somewhere in the rock where we cannot get to her. But add rabid shifters into the mix?

We are way out of our element on this island. I try not to harbor guilt from having to knock out Jaime, but I cannot allow an attack to slow me down. Santiago has waited for me to save him from Máximo long enough.

When I reach the others, Tio Bruno and Rafael are staring at the volcano. Rafi's got his arms crossed, looking like a soldier sizing up an enemy. Tio Bruno's hands are pressed to the black rocky wall, making him look like a man on the edge of his sanity.

Dating Tavita is going to be complicated for Tio Bruno if he can't hold it together this long without her.

Not like I'm one to talk. I haven't seen Adelita in days, and her absence tears at my stomach lining. I'm hollow inside, and not just because I'm hungry and tired from too much effort and not enough food. I know for certain that if she was here, I would be able to move forward more easily. If only I could have brought her with me.

But that would have been foolish. Adelita deserves more than my selfish nature that would keep her close forever. A little space is good.

It also feels like murder in my soul.

"A cadejo," I tell the guys once I'm close enough and can catch my breath. "It's a shifter like I've never seen before, just like Tavita said. His animal is a monster called Chupacabra. Máximo is trying to erase his humanity so the man is only and always the monster."

Tio Bruno grimaces, recoiling from my words. "That's horrible. I didn't know mutations like that were possible. I thought you controlled your animal, not the other way around."

"We do. Máximo has messed with something he should not have touched."

Rafael nods once. "Fine. It's an animal. That's easy

enough. If any come near, we'll be able to defend the perimeter, no problem."

I shake my head. "No, Rafi. It's not a normal animal. It's got long claws and a fin on its back with spikes. It's hairless and sort of looks like a giant canine with a cat's tail, mixed with a deadly lizard. The one I caught out there shifted halfway. He couldn't get back to his human self. It was big, and the teeth were sharper than any knives we've managed to hang onto out here. The sooner we get out of here, the better. Our best bet is to hope we go unnoticed."

Rafi's jaw tightens. "Did you kill it?"

I stand by his side. "No. He's a man in captivity. He's afraid of his Chupacabra, Rafi. He can't control it. If he attacks, it's not his choosing. I've never met a cadejo who wasn't one with his animal. I knocked him out, but I'm sure not how long that will last, or which side of himself he'll be when he wakes."

Rafi closes his eyes. "Awesome."

We stand a few feet behind Tio Bruno in silence, watching his body tense as he palms the volcano, as if willing himself to draw Tavita out of nature's prison with his hands and sheer will. When he sinks to his knees, his gait is off, but he manages to lower his body without removing his hands from the hard surface. "Leave us, Rafi. I need a word with Santos."

Rafael looks at me curiously, to which I shrug but nod. "Don't wander far. And keep your steps quiet," I warn him.

What could Tio Bruno possibly want to say to me that he can't say in front of Rafi?

I don't approach Tio Bruno after Rafi trots away, but speak to him from where I stand a little way behind. "I'm listening, Commander."

Tio Bruno's head bows. "How do you live like this? How are you composed?"

My head tilts to the side. "What do you mean?"

"Tavita might be in danger, and it's all I can do not to tear this thing apart to get at her. From the first day you met Adelita, she's been in danger from the Kalku, from Máximo. How are you not a wreck right now? I feel deranged, like my insides are splintering apart."

I rub my chest. "I know that feeling well. I've been at this longer than you have. That helps. Also, I know Adelita is with Cruz. There's no safer place than by his side." My voice lowers. "But make no mistake, Tio Bruno. I am not composed, and no part of me feels alive when she is far from me."

"La Ciguapa is tearing me up. I'm going insane thinking what might be happening to her in there."

My lips purse as I try to put words to the truth. "The magic can't matter. La Ciguapa or not, magic or not,

Máximo or not, the Kalku or not, I would choose Adelita. She is good to me, even when there's nothing good *in* me. She listens well and isn't afraid to speak up. She understands me even when I don't know myself. I don't care if her being La Ciguapa, or her incredible magic, or Máximo or the Kalku add to that or not. Adelita is who I love. Everything else just adds intensity."

Tio Bruno nods vigorously. "That's what's scaring me. It doesn't worry me that I care for Tavita. That part feels right to me. She's a good person. Independent and funny. Tough and smart. It makes sense why any man would fall head over heels for her. It's the intensity of it all that's shaking my bones up."

I mull over his conundrum. "I understand that completely. Breathe through it, Commander. She doesn't want this for you—this falling apart and not being able to stand on your own. Tavita is a good woman who doesn't want you on your knees. If she's anything like her sister, then Tavita will only ever build you up." I pause to study the height of the volcano, which seems to stretch to the sky. "So give her what she wants. She wants you to be able to let her go on a mission without you falling apart. She wants to be useful to Cáceres. Keeping her in a plastic bubble to shield her from the world would crush her spirit." I move to Tio Bruno's side and offer him my hand. "Build each other up and let her fight for what she wants in her own way. To clip her wings because it keeps her safe in your hand is cruel."

Tio Bruno frowns up at me. "Cruel?"

I help him up with a hefty hoist. "You cannot be selfish with La Ciguapa, or your passion for her will eat you alive."

"It's already happening," Tio Bruno chokes out. It's strange to see him so consumed by anything other than his usual purpose of looking after the village. Had I not diverted some of Adelita's affections, I wonder if this is how Cruz would have turned out.

I take a chance and put my hand on my commander's shoulder. He may be my superior, but in this, we are brothers. "I will not let you disappear. That means you have to listen to me."

Tio Bruno draws in a long breath, adjusting to this new dynamic between us. "Okay. Yes. I'm listening, Santos."

"Is there anything you can do for her right now?"

"Nothing!" His reply has such a mournful quality to it that my heart stutters. I know his angst, for it is my own.

I nod once, looking him dead in the eye. "Then go to Rafi. Walk with him and get some air. Practice being without Tavita, even if it's only for a few minutes, a few yards. You will do her no good if you keep carrying on like this. Good women do not want to be a man's obsession. That is not love. She wants to be your partner, your teammate. So no more groveling on your knees." I hate the next words that come from me, but they must be said. "Addiction is not love. Need is not love. Love her well. That means you scout the perimeter. And instead of dwelling on the fact that you're worried about her right now, think up ways to keep Cáceres safe when we get back."

Tio Bruno's frown lines deepen. "I don't like this."

With as little attitude as I can muster, I take the reins of the conversation, drawing myself up so I seem more intimidating. "I don't care. She did not fall for a man who cannot defend his household. She fell for a soldier. Be yourself, or she will have no reason to stay."

That shakes him into place. His chin lowers, and I can see how out of his element he truly is in all of this. "Okay. You'll watch this spot? Listen well. If she gets stuck in the walls, maybe you'll be able to hear her."

I press the flat of my hand to my sternum. "Yes, Commander."

At my formal address, Tio Bruno finally remembers himself. He trots off with some semblance of purpose and a slice of confidence. It gives me hope that he will be alright, and won't lose himself completely. I'll just have to keep a better eye on him.

I wonder if this is how Cruz felt looking after me.

I rest my ear against the wall, noting the cool rock. I wonder when the volcano erupted last. I've never heard of it doing a single thing in my lifetime, other than holding the Luz Mala.

The quiet of the night is unsettling. There's no trace of wildlife. No birds chirping, no insects making their presence known.

The wind whistles, and I wonder if Máximo knows he has visitors.

As if nature can read my thoughts, a shadow falls over the island, bathing it in a truer darkness than existed before. A chill creeps over my skin, causing goosebumps to splinter over my arms.

Rafi's gasp from a stone's throw away jerks my head in his direction. He's looking into the sky near the mouth of the volcano, his jaw dropped in astonishment.

I follow his gaze and realize why the sky turned black.

It wasn't a cloud crossing the moon. It wasn't the thought of Máximo that turned the sky black.

The Luz Mala has gone out.

My eyes comb the base of the volcano, searching for

signs of Tavita as Rafi and Tio Bruno come charging toward the spot where I stand.

"She did it!" Rafi whispers. "She found the Luz Mala. It didn't dawn on me that the light would be gone when she takes it through the side of the volcano. Duh." Rafael rolls his eyes at himself.

Tio Bruno presses his palm to the rock, again willing her to come to him. "Right here, Tavita. Fight through the wall. Come back to me."

As if on command, Tavita stumbles out of the rock two feet down from where I stand, as if she's stepped through a wrinkled veil.

Shirtless.

She's carrying her shirt in one arm and the Luz Mala in the other, wrapped in... Did she wrap the Luz Mala in her sock?

I'm not sure what I was expecting the Luz Mala to be. Even though we sent her in to get it, part of me imagined the source of Máximo's magic to be ethereal and ungraspable. But when my eyes fall on the token in Tavita's possession, it takes me a second to compute that the handful of emeralds look no more impressive than a few oddly shaped marbles.

Such trinkets, such small things, yet they have been the source of so much strife.

They are not glowing anymore, telling me that the

light of Máximo's immortality has finally gone out from the world.

He is mostly mortal now, and ripe for the killing.

My mouth goes dry. "We have to destroy the emeralds when we get back to the mainland. I don't think anything here is strong enough to crush them to powder."

"But the light has gone out," Tavita argues. "That's gotta mean it's done."

I shake my head. It may be lore I'm clinging to, but it's led us this far, so I trust it. "Máximo can be killed, but his spirit will not move on from this realm until the Luz Mala is completely destroyed. That includes crushing the emeralds. Grind them down to nothing, or Máximo's spirit will not move on."

Rafi winces. "Yikes. But we can kill him now?"

I nod once. "We should be able to, yes."

Tio Bruno couldn't care less about the Luz Mala right now. Tavita's clad in only jeans and a bra. It's clear he's torn between lust and horror that we're seeing her like this.

She's winded, and sets her shirt on the sand with a lengthy huff. Upon closer inspection, I can see it's filled with something. Rocks, maybe, that she brought out from the heart of the volcano, transported in the material of her top. "Hey, guys. Could I borrow a shirt? I used mine to carry out a ton of gold and jewels that were inside the volcano." She grins up with pride over her plunder. "That should cover my expenses and Adelita's in Cáceres, right?"

My nose scrunches. "Adelita has no living expenses. She lives with us. Whatever she needs, I'll provide."

Tio Bruno frowns in time with me. "Who said anything about living expenses? Those have been covered."

Tavita's mouth twists to the side. I can tell she's battling with her words, trying to pick the correct ones. "And we appreciate that. But at some point, we want to be able to stand on our own. Contribute instead of take."

Tio Bruno rips his shirt over his head and helps her put it on. "Whatever makes you happy, Blue Eyes. Keep your treasure." He rubs his hands up and down her biceps, connecting with her body. "Are you alright?"

She grins at us. "Never better. We did it. The Luz Mala has been put out. The second I touched the emeralds where the light was coming from, they went out. No wonder Máximo had them so protected in there. These emeralds are coming home with us. Máximo can live out the rest of his miserable days without them."

Rafi's fingers are careful as he reaches out and pokes the emeralds. "Trippy. They look so normal now."

"Do you think anyone noticed the light going out?" I glance over my shoulder, but still there's nothing.

Too much nothing.

Rafi's brows pinch together. "Not to be a buzzkill, but how are we going to rescue Santiago with no light? When you were in the walls of the volcano with it, the whole sky went dark. I'm surprised no one's coming to check on it."

None of us has a plan for this, judging by the silence that greets Rafi's concern.

Tavita's voice is quiet but firm. "This is our one chance to finally cut Máximo's reign short."

My knees bend and I put my body between the others and whatever just made a noise out there. "Something heard us." Before whatever it is reaches us, I lock eyes with Rafi. "If I don't make it out of this, promise me you'll free Santiago and explain things to Adelita."

Rafi moves to stand at my side, his knife drawn. "I will watch you, brother. Everything is going to be okay. Santiago will not die on this island. You have my word."

"Santos!" comes a voice in the distance.

We all stiffen until the call comes again. My shoulders relax. "It's the cadejo from earlier." When Jaime comes into view on two legs, fully human, I nod. "Hello, Jaime."

"Tavita?" Jaime runs to her and throws his arms

around Tavita. "No! You have to get out of here. You know Máximo only let you escape because he wanted you to bring your sister here. Tell me you found a way to resist! Tell me she's not here!"

Tavita squeezes Jaime like two old friends who have been through a war together. "They took out the implant so Máximo can't control me anymore. I'm here to get you out, Jaime. Everyone. We are taking Máximo out tonight. The Luz Mala is destroyed."

Jaime pulls back, his eyes drifting to the emeralds in Tavita's hand. "Is that... How did you... Everyone else is sleeping. I think I'm the only one who saw the beam of light go out." He gapes at her. "You did it. You actually went through the volcano's wall. I didn't think it possible." Then Jaime grimaces. "My monster wants to run back to Máximo and tell him right now. You can't let me do that! Hurry!" His head whips from side to side. "Santiago would be able to calm my animal down. You have to help me! Don't let me ruin this for us!"

My heart swells with affection for Jaime because of his praise of my brother. Still, a creeping presence laces through my body. I don't know its intent, but I'm more on edge than I care to be. "Let's go, then. Can you lead the way?"

Jaime nods in short jerks. "You have to stay here,

Tavita. If Máximo sees you, it's all over. I'll take the others, but you need to stay away."

Tavita holds the emeralds to her chest, tucking her body into Tio Bruno's side. "I can do that. Bruno, will you stay with me?"

Tio Bruno doesn't need to be asked twice. "Of course." He reaches down and slides a knife out of his boot. "You'll need this, Santos."

I take my commander's only weapon and turn toward Jaime. "Tell your animal that you're taking us to Máximo. That should pacify him for now."

Jaime exhales with relief. "Thank you." Then he turns and starts off at a run, leading the way toward Máximo's home.

Toward Santiago.

Toward freedom.

6

GOING TO BED WITH CRUZ
ADELITA

I rub my hand across my stomach. "I can't remember the last time I had that much stew. Did you put apples in it?"

Salvador's eyes dance with satisfaction. "I did. I'm glad you liked it. I'm sure you're used to fancier food in Cáceres, but down here, we like to perfect the simple things."

"Well, I can't imagine it getting better than that." I glance at the pot in the middle of the table, slightly crestfallen that there's no more of the delicious food left.

Cruz slides his bowl over to me. "I can't finish mine."

"What a sweet little liar you are."

Cruz smirks at me. "I had a bowl and a half. That's more than enough."

Cruz is twice my size, so I know that's not true.

I pick up the spoon and take a bite, but the next one I feed to Cruz. We're one of those sickly affectionate couples now, I guess, and that fact doesn't bother me one bit. Cruz dips his head closer to me, his breath perfumed with the succulent beef broth and sweet apples. He really shouldn't sit this close to me. It's hard to fight off the urge to suck on his lower lip.

Maybe it's just that I'm coming down from the tension of the day or perhaps it's the wine, but for whatever reason, my entire body is relaxed now. I love leaning my shoulder to his, sharing the bowl of stew. His nose brushes across mine when he goes in for the next bite. I'm fairly certain the blush in my cheeks could be seen from space, were we not underground.

I want this man so very badly.

Eva and Salvador are mired in their hushed back-and-forth, which I can only catch odd hints of. Phrases like "That's not policy," "You should know better," and "But that's not what you love about me," hit my ears. I make quick work of spooning out the last of the stew.

Eva and Salvador are going to be debating who knows what for the entire night, I'm guessing. That's not how I want to spend my time. "Tired," I tell Cruz, tugging lightly on his wrist.

"So tired," Cruz echoes with a boyish grin. "Thanks,

Salvador. If you're thinking of eavesdropping again tonight, I wouldn't."

I guffaw at his innuendo, though it's exactly spot on.

"Enjoy your plunder," Salvador calls.

Cruz frowns at him. "I didn't steal her. She's not a thing."

"I was talking to Adelita."

I mime a laugh and lead Cruz down the hall. "Don't engage with him. He'll be your brother-in-law soon enough, so best pace yourself. Dealing with Salvador might be a lifelong exercise in learning patience."

Cruz stops short. "Don't even joke about that. You think my dad is cool? Wait until he catches wind of that. You'll see where my thunder really comes from."

"I don't want to talk about Salvador. I don't want to talk at all." I shut the bedroom door behind us and lean against it.

Cruz doesn't need the rest spelled out for him. Though both Santos and Cruz have made it clear they have limited experience with women, Cruz is no stranger to taking control. Two fingers trace down the slope of my cheek, lingering on my jaw so he can tilt my head however it pleases him.

If he thinks he can torture me by going painfully slow, he has no idea how badly I want him.

My lips are impatient, and find his without the usual hesitation that comes from testing the waters of a new relationship. My fingers twine in his hair as I stand on my toes, pulling him closer because I'm utterly starved for this man. There are always too many fires to put out, too many lives to save, but this is exactly what I crave for this slice of a moment where all we have to do is stay put.

I love the taste of him, and don't bother holding back the noises of contentment that come from kissing his full lips. He follows my lead, giving in to my harried pace, even though I'm pretty sure he wanted to take his time teasing me.

I'm too aware of how easily our moments can be snatched away from us, so I don't want to go slow tonight. This night is ours, and I'm not about to tiptoe through it.

Cruz's pulse thumps under my fingertips when they graze his throat, tracing down his cut torso and dipping down to his belly. A thrill runs through me as I lift up the hem of his shirt, revealing the scandal of his beautiful torso to the air. He smells like home and looks like a fantasy I never dreamed I'd be able to touch. My hands take their chance with perfection, stroking and manhandling every inch of flesh he exposes to me. Though I've seen him shirtless loads of times, tonight, I'm hungry for the sight of him completely uncovered.

My heels hit the ground as my mouth drags down his chest so I can kiss a line over his sternum. His pulse is thundering now, announcing that this is exactly where he wants to be. My tongue flicks over his nipple while my fingernails toy with the other. His gasps are heady. I collect them all so I can keep the parts of him I love the most.

His vulnerability is what I crave. This undressed, unprotected part of him that gives itself over to me with each shaky breath he cannot tame.

I would never want this great man tamed. I want him exactly as he is, shivering with need before me just like this.

As I lower myself to kiss my way down his stomach, he grips the bottom of my shirt and peels it over my head. Our shoes kick off, my toes curling in the packed dirt floor as he tugs me back up so he can ravage my mouth with his tongue. His kiss is more forceful now, and my body compliant to this beast I've awoken. When his arm reaches around to unhook my bra, no part of me wants to be anywhere but here. His tongue is devious, teasing and taking with such confidence that by the time he lowers me to the bed, I am a puddle of need, begging for more.

When his jeans fall to the floor, my knees part, inviting him in—always inviting. We've held back for too long; our bodies won't tolerate being denied another second. Cruz lowers himself atop me on the mattress, kissing me hard as he pops open the button of my jeans. His lips draw a scorching line from my mouth down to my breasts, where he nips and tugs until I'm frantically clawing at the sheets. It's like his mouth belongs suctioned to my body. My back arches for him and my skin sings while incoherent desire scrapes out of my throat. Though I thought I could conduct the pace of our tryst, Cruz would never truly surrender control.

How I love this man.

"I need you, Cruz. Please!"

He chuckles into my navel, then licks a few inches below just to torture me. "So impatient. It would be cruel to tease you any longer, wouldn't it."

"So cruel!" My hips bump upward, seeking friction he won't give me.

He chuckles darkly and slows his pace, dragging his lips to my wrist so he can suck at a snail's pace.

Everything about him is warm and inviting. The feel of his body heat connecting with mine is just about the best feeling in the world. There is nothing I would not do for this man. He was so gruff and abrasive in the beginning, but now he is considerate in the way he regards me.

His lips move slowly down my throat, sucking and

biting and utterly indulging in every part of me that has been exposed to him. We've worked so hard.

Now it's time to play.

My eyes roll into the back of my head at the sensation of his prickly jaw atop my sternum. I'm fairly certain I'm teetering on the edge of deranged, but Cruz doesn't care. He loves me like this—craving him above all else.

When his fingers tickle a line across my breast, I cry out for more. "Please!"

"Did you really think it would be that quick? I'm going to take my time tonight. I'm going to enjoy this for hours. If you're very lucky, I'll let you enjoy this, too."

I whimper, utterly pathetic in my need for him. But my plea does nothing as Cruz makes good on his word.

Over the next three hours, Cruz takes his sweet time drawing out every ounce of pleasure from my body, tormenting me until we're both completely and utterly spent.

As long as I live, I will never doubt the love I have for this man.

7

THE LOCKED HALLWAY
ADELITA

I can't believe anything rouses me in the middle of the night, but apparently my bladder isn't willing to negotiate with the protest from my boneless limbs. After slipping out from under Cruz's covetous hold on my breast even in slumber, I tug on my jeans and hoodie and pad my way down the hall.

When I make my way back to the bedroom, a shadow emerges from the darkness.

"Eva? Is that you?"

Eva shrinks at being called out. She presses her finger to her lips and holds up a set of keys she's got clutched in her fist.

"What are you doing?" I whisper, suddenly wide awake.

"What you've been thinking of doing since Salvador mentioned the hallway we're not allowed to go down."

"What?" Alarm bells ring through my brain. "Eva, no. Salvador is allowed to have a messy closet he doesn't want us to see. This is his home. Boundaries are healthy."

Eva tilts her head at me as if she's certain I've lost my mind. "If the secrets of a crowned prince are so bad that they need to be locked up, that's not a good sign."

"Put his keys back, Eva. Seriously. He's helping us out. I thought you liked him."

Guilt flashes over her features. "I do. Was it that obvious?"

I don't know how to answer that. "If you like Salvador, then grant him his privacy."

Panic climbs in her eyes as we stand in the hallway like two little girls afraid of waking their parents. "Because I like him, I *have* to do this! I have to know what he's hiding, or I can't go down this road. I have to know what's wrong with him so I can write him off, like I have all the others. I need a reason not to be with him."

"I mean, him locking us up to extract information is a good place to start," I mutter. Then I remember my profession and take a calming breath. "If you're looking this hard to sabotage something you clearly want, then maybe you aren't ready for it. Happiness is a hard pill for a lot of people to swallow. You have to want to be happy, to choose it. Right now, you're choosing mistrust. You're choosing to dig for some reason to keep yourself from the man you clearly want. Why do you think that is?"

Eva lowers her head, but then a second later snaps it back up with a glower. "I know what you're doing. You're mind-melding me with your therapy talk. I'm not living under a roof that has a secret in plain sight."

When a man's voice interrupts us, I startle with a squeak. "Nor should you," Salvador says, strolling into the hallway. He's wearing dark green pajama pants and a tired smile. "Apologies, Lady Eva. I didn't realize my privacy was such a threat to your sanity. Allow me." He takes his keys from her hand and strides toward the forbidden zone.

Eva's neck shrinks. Then she glances at me and shrugs.

I guess we're going to find out the big secret after all.

All of us freeze when the sounds of a fight hit our ears. I spin on my heel when I realize the voice belongs to Cruz, and waste no time darting into our bedroom.

Salvador and Eva trail into our bedroom after me, standing near the entrance while I climb into the bed beside Cruz. "Shh," I coo, smoothing my fingers down his bristly cheek. "I'm here."

Cruz's body was rife with tension, but at my touch,

he calms, his spine sinking into the lumpy mattress. His defenseless whimper breaks my heart. He cuddles into my body, nuzzling his nose to my neck so I can be his shelter through his nightly storms.

I caress his arm. With every pass over his muscle, I hope I'm wiping his troubles away.

"It's alright. I won't leave you alone." It's a promise that's easy to keep, so I make it freely and often. Even though I'm fairly certain he's still asleep, the vow rings true.

I love the feel of his breath on my skin.

Eva flicks on the light, drawing out a cringe from us both. "Let's go, lovebirds. Salvador's about to make the skeletons in his closet dance for us."

Cruz's lashes flutter against my jaw as he slowly pieces the world together. "Did... Did you leave?"

"Bathroom," I admit. "I'm sorry you were alone."

Cruz kisses my neck and then rolls onto his back, the sheet falling to his bare waist. "Eva? What are you doing here?"

"Averting my eyes and waiting for you to get up and get dressed. Salvador's got a surprise for us."

"What time is it?"

I kiss Cruz's forehead and then snatch up his jeans from the floor, handing them to him. "It's the middle of the night. Eva won't be able to sleep until she sees what's lurking down Salvador's locked hallway."

Cruz rolls his eyes at his sister as he pulls on his pants. "Honestly, Eva."

Eva doesn't shrink at the mild scolding. "I'm certain he's hiding something important. I'm going off my gut here, Cruz."

Salvador appears mildly amused, but there's a sadness in his eyes that's unmistakable. "You're right, as usual. Perhaps it's good you were snooping. I was afraid to show you the truth, but the whole thing is growing out of my control. I could use some help, actually." Salvador meets her eyes with kindness. "Never question your gut. Let's go have a look, shall we?"

Eva, though mollified, still huffs with indignation even as she takes his arm and strides down the corridor by his side.

"Those two are going to give me an ulcer," Cruz mumbles. He always looks gruff, but woken mid-sleep after a brief bout with La Sayona, his face is positively surly.

But I know the softy that lies beneath, so I don't hesitate to cuddle into his side while we follow behind the odd pair. "I kind of like them. Eva needs someone who will keep her interested. Salvador will challenge her and listen to her, it seems like. I dunno. They're growing on me."

Cruz grumbles incoherently, so I rub his belly while we walk. I miss Santos horribly, so I cling tighter to Cruz.

"He'll be okay," Cruz whispers as we walk through the living room.

"I didn't say anything."

"I know, but I figured you were thinking about Santos. He'll be fine. He'll come back to us without a scratch on him. I wouldn't have let him go if I wasn't certain of it. He and Rafi will be back."

I stop so I can stare up at him. "How did you know I was thinking about Santos?"

Cruz shrugs. "Just a hunch. My gut is as loud as Eva's, apparently."

We're so entwined now that moments like these where he accidentally reads my mind startle me. "I'm grateful for you, you know."

He ducks down and kisses me. There's a reverence to the way he holds my face with one hand, the slow slip of his lips against mine. He loves me. I can taste it in his kiss. Though Salvador and Eva are fiddling with the lock already, my feet have no desire to move from this spot.

Cruz's lips are soft, surrounded by his prickly facial

hair that always begs for a shaving. He tastes like a man who isn't afraid to go after what he wants, even though that's one of the reasons we took so long to get together. Now there's a settled boldness to him that I adore and can't get enough of.

It takes Eva whistling to regain our attention. She taps her foot, her hand on her hip. "Big reveal over here, guys. Make babies on your own time." A twinkle sparks in her eyes the second the words slip out of her mouth. "Auntie Eva. I like that."

That knocks the sense back into me. "Sorry, guys. We're still waking up." I tangle my fingers through Cruz's, remembering the reason for being out of bed.

Salvador doesn't turn down the hallway, but watches us as we approach. There's a wistfulness to him in lieu of his usual teasing expression. "I really like the two of you together."

"Well, that's good, because that's how we come."

Salvador fixes his gaze on Cruz. "That's a relief. I get the feeling I would loathe you if Adelita wasn't here to soften you. Maybe the stories of La Ciguapa aren't all that bad."

I cast Salvador a withering look. "Wow, thanks."

Salvador stands in the passageway, which doesn't have drywall like the rest of the house. The floor and walls are packed dirt, but the floor has a few large rocks scattered over it, each big enough to need light to ensure they can be stepped over without falling. Salvador rubs the nape of his neck, clutching his keys a little too hard. "I took one of your big secrets without your permission, so this is one I'm giving to you, so you don't feel the need to sneak around in the middle of the night to steal it. I want things between our tribes to be better, but that won't happen if you can't trust me. And it really won't happen if I don't trust you with my biggest sin."

Yikes. Biggest sin? I don't like the sound of that at all. He doesn't owe us this sort of information. I can't let this be how we interact. "Salvador, I forgive you. You don't have to do this if you don't want. You have a right to your privacy, and you've let us in more than most. You letting us stay here and hide out is all it takes to build a healthy bridge between the two tribes."

Salvador's shoulders lower. "Truthfully, I'm in over my head. There aren't many who might be able to understand the tight situation I've found myself in. I could use your help. All three of you."

Cruz scrubs his hand over his face. "I need coffee or something. How awake do I have to be for this?"

Salvador doesn't answer, but leads the way silently, holding tight to Eva's hand to help her over the trickier spots. He accommodates her movements easily, even holding her waist to assist her in hopping over one of the larger boulders.

When we reach the end of the hallway, there's another locked door. Salvador moves slowly as he selects the correct key and slides it into the knob. "This is my greatest crime." Then he opens the door, flicks on a light, leading us inside.

The cold creeps down my spine, forcing a shiver of trepidation through me. My eyes fall on a lifeless man, perhaps in his late sixties, lying on a frameless mattress on the ground in the corner. There's an IV and a few other tubes surround his slumbering body.

Eva gasps, her hand flying over her mouth. "Salvador, is that..."

Salvador looks older now, tired beyond his years. "That's my father. Everyone in Anzaldúa thinks he has simply become a recluse in his advancing years. The truth of it all is far darker than that." He meets Eva's eyes with a culpable look. "I did this. The reason my father is locked in here is because of me."

Fear rips through me as the light flickers and then fades to darkness.

8

SANTIAGO
SANTOS

I shift halfway to Máximo's home because my wolf runs far better than I do on two legs. Though Jaime, Rafi and I are all shifters, Rafi's dragon isn't exactly inconspicuous, and Jaime's monster is, well, an uncontrollable monster.

Jaime keeps feeding us information while we run, and I know each morsel costs him greatly. I can hear the strain in his voice as he struggles to help us without angering his Chupacabra too much. "The slaves sleep in the barn over there to the right. The only people in the house are Máximo, and sometimes Santiago, if Máximo's having trouble sleeping."

I hate that my brother's hauntingly beautiful voice has been used to lull that psychopath to sleep.

"There are two boats at the dock over there. You

have to leave us behind, though."

That request makes me trip over my paws. I recover my stride and send up a confused yip.

Jaime clarifies. "All of us have had our animals messed with, except for Santiago. Take him, but leave the rest of us to die here. We cannot be around other people. Our Chupacabras belong to Máximo alone. We would be a terror on the mainland. We would all run straight for our families, but then we'd shift at the wrong time. It's a disaster waiting to happen. Let us die on the island. It's the only way to save the rest of the world from us."

Rafael answers for the both of us. "We're not leaving you here. That's not an option. We'll take you all back to Cáceres, where we live. We'll sedate you if we have to so we have time to work up a cure."

I shift onto two legs, which is problematic to do while sprinting. The team slows after I faceplant, and Rafi helps me to my feet.

I'm panting, but the words make their way into the air. "We know someone who can cure a shifter's wounded animal."

Rafi casts me a worried look. "That's an overpromise, Santos. We don't know if Adelita can actually fix them."

"She fixed your dragon," I point out.

"Yeah, but my dragon was underdeveloped, not

rabid. It's not the same thing."

I shrug. "Well, it's worth a shot. If it doesn't work, the healers can do their thing and try to undo it. Leaving Máximo's victims here isn't on the table for discussion."

Rafi nods. "That part, I'll agree with."

Jaime shakes his head. "Our monsters will come out the second we get out on the water. A few tried to escape that way, and it always ends poorly. Our Chupacabras are loyal to Máximo. They don't want to be separate from him."

My mouth pulls to the side. "We'll have to knock you all out, then. It's the only way. We didn't cross the waters just to give up because it's going to be hard."

Jaime pauses to puzzle through my suggestion, and then throws his arms around me, holding me in a tight hug. "That will work. Thank you, Don Santos."

I scramble away from the affection and the name that indicates reverence and respect. "I'm not Don Santos. I'm Santos. I'm no one."

Jaime won't be dissuaded. "You're saving us at great personal risk. You are Don Santos."

Rafi grins at me with a silent giggle. "I like that. Much better than Santos the Savage."

We keep up a moderate pace as we near the barn. My eyes search the grounds for Santiago, but there is no one sitting or lying outside the large hut's rickety gate.

My stomach drops when I come to grips with the possibility that my brother is inside with Máximo. Going in will be far more risky, sure, but having to see him singing to that criminal isn't something my stomach can handle. I need to get him out of here now. Even though we have a plan, I'm frantic to get to my twin. I've been fractured for too long without him. The prospect of finally being whole gnaws at my bones, begging me to move into the house to retrieve my lost brother.

The hair on my arms stands on end as we lurk toward the house. As much as I want to free the others, I cannot be parted from my brother another minute.

Whether Rafi agrees with my direction or not, he doesn't question it, but shadows me because that's what we do. If it's Cruz that's going off on a hunch or a dogged need, we protect him. I'm not often the one calling the shots, but Rafi supports my whims, knowing me well enough to understand that this is what I need to do.

Jaime's whisper is terse and laced with trepidation. "Máximo's bedroom is to the left. Santiago's wolf hasn't been messed with, so he'll let you enter without a fight. My Chupacabra isn't going to like any of this, so I'll go wait in the barn with the others."

Rafi cups Jaime's shoulder. "Finish line, friend."

Jaime's smile has a note of pain to it.

I know the feeling well. Hoping for freedom is agony.

Jamie nods once. "Finish line."

We part ways, which gives me a modicum of confidence. This is what I'm used to—going on missions with Rafi. This is normal. Boring, even. At least, that's what I tell myself as we sneak through the gate and enter in through the back door. There are no locks on the entrance, which bespeaks of cockiness, and a faultless trust placed in Massacooramaan.

I can understand that. I have absolute faith in Rafael and Cruz. If they are guarding me, I know there's nothing to fear.

That's when it dawns on me that we are surely going to succeed—not because our mission is righteous, but because my brother is by my side. Rafael will not let me fail; he loves me too much.

I reach back and grab his wrist, then I sign a quick, *"I'm glad you're with me."*

Though I can tell Rafi is anxious by the tension in his gait, he crosses his eyes and gives me a goofy grin, signing, *"I'm going to drive Santiago nuts, aren't I."*

A wry smile splits my face. *"I'm counting on it."* I can picture perfectly Santiago getting exasperated with Rafi's antics, but saying nothing because he's been raised to believe that speaking up for yourself isn't allowed.

Rafael did the same thing with me when I was newer to Cáceres. He told endless jokes, all with "fart" being the punchline. It was so irritating that one day, I finally snapped and asked him to tell any other joke, please.

I remember his smile perfectly. His grin was wide and he clapped me on the shoulder. "Finally. You voiced an opinion. My work here is done."

But Rafael's work to bring Santiago out of his shell will begin soon enough. Rafi's medicine is necessary, and I'm grateful he is my brother.

My chest swells as we move stealthily through the bare hut. I'll get to teach Santiago how to use his voice. He'll get to learn how to have an opinion.

I'm enamored of the prospect of assimilating Santiago into my life. *Our* life.

I have to remind myself to focus. One wrong step and we could wake Máximo before we have a chance to kill him.

The hut is wooden and empty, as far as furniture goes. When we round the corner, there is a table and one chair. I guess Máximo wouldn't have a need for a second, given that he's enslaved everyone here. He is missing out completely on the notion of dining with a friend.

The sight saddens me. It is power at its most foolish.

Máximo's friend who followed him to this island has been mutated to the point where they cannot dine together. There is no chair for the Massacooramaan. Máximo's lust for power left no room at his table for a brother.

The hut isn't huge, but it takes some navigating, especially since we're in the dark. I want to find Santiago quicker than this, so I take a chance and close my eyes, willing my soul to find its lost mate. Maybe that's silly and superstitious, but it's the best compass I've got at the moment.

When I tap into my inner map, my feet itch to turn left through the dining area, which leads us to a short hallway with a single room off to the side.

It's not the doorway that catches my breath, but the sight of my brother sleeping on the floor in the hallway. His hair is long and unwashed, his torso bare. The second I think that, a shiver rolls through my twin, yanking at my heart.

He has not been cared for. He's filthy, for one, and he's wearing shorts so dirty and thin, I can't imagine how little it would take to tear them. My bulk is more substantial than his now. Santiago is too thin for my liking. It's clear Chef Aarón takes good care of the people he feeds. I've been utterly spoiled while my brother has been neglected.

We are identical, so it's not just Santiago I see, lying unkempt on the floor; it's myself I see, as well.

Rafael stays still at the end of the hallway, nudging me forward.

My mouth is dry and my palms sweaty as I tiptoe toward my slumbering twin. I will my knees not to creak as I kneel beside his slumbering form. My fingers hesitate before they touch lightly on Santiago's cheek, tracing down the side of his face. Santiago leans into the touch in his sleep. I wonder how long it's been since anyone has been gentle to him.

I don't realize I'm crying until tears splash onto the floor, marking just how deep I've been burying my loneliness after losing my only biological family.

When Santiago's lashes flutter, my face is the first thing he sees. He smiles, and then goes back to sleep, no doubt thinking he's having a dream about me.

I pinch his cheek, drawing him to wakefulness. This time, his eyes widen when he sees me and puts it together that this is all real, and not a happy dream. Santiago's mouth pops open, relief flooding his face before it is quickly replaced by terror. He sits up, gripping my shoulders in earnest.

My finger presses perpendicular to my lips, reminding him to be silent. I bring my face to his ear and whisper, "We're getting you out and killing Máximo."

Santiago's fingers squeeze my arms, like he's afraid if he slackens his grip, I'll vanish before his eyes. "Are you real, Brother?"

No matter the urgency, our hug cannot be delayed another second. There's a familiarity that sweeps over me, a memory attached to a thousand others that trickles over my skin with the tug of a million tears. "I am real, Santiago, and I am here. We've come to get you out."

Santiago shudders against me. His skin has a lingering chill to it that makes me loathe Máximo all the more. "Santos," he says with unconcealed mourning in his whisper.

I kiss my twin's cheek and motion to Rafi, whose eyes are wet as he stands a few feet away. "This is Rafael. He is going to take you and the others to safety while I finish off Máximo. Go with him."

Santiago digs his fingers into my arms, pulling back so he can glimpse my face in the dark. "No! You cannot kill him. It cannot be done. Believe me, if it could, I would have succeeded. There is a dark magic about him that's weakened me each time I've tried. It's killed some of the others he's enslaved. No, Santos. Do not even think about it."

My eyes close in frustration. "Of course he would guard against common assaults. If trying to kill him weakens me, I might not be able to get you home."

"Home? You have a home?" Santiago's tears slick his cheeks. "I hoped, but I couldn't know for certain. They've taken you in?"

"Us," I assure him. "They've taken *us* in. It's your home, too."

Rafi jerks his head toward the exit, silently reminding us we're catching up on borrowed time.

I loathe every step I take that leads me away from my prey. Máximo captured Adelita's sister and tried to kidnap my love right out of my arms. He stole my brother and countless other people's brothers. A swift death is a kindness, and I would give him exactly that.

But I know Santiago, and he is telling the truth. He fears for my life if I try this, and I have a woman back home who is expecting me to return. Revenge is not an even trade for my life, no matter how tempting that may be.

I cringe when the door creaks on our way out, but there's no sign of stirring in the hut.

Santiago in the moonlight is an incredible sight. I can't stop staring at my brother and the changes two years have made. His features are gaunt and positively haunted, but he's upright. There's still a fire in his eyes that assures me the source of our mischief has not gone out completely.

Santiago points at a band on his ankle. "It shocks me if Máximo is displeased."

I nod once. "Then it must come off."

"I've tried! Once my knife touches it, a current runs through my hand, as well."

Rafael takes charge. "I'm on it. Hold still."

I have no idea what Rafi's plan is, but I don't bother to ask questions.

Rafael blows out a long breath, and I watch his arm transform from the umber flesh to the olive-scaled limb that belongs to his dragon. The change doesn't affect him more than just his arm. I'm so proud of the control he's learning.

The long claw isn't graceful, but it doesn't slice Santiago's leg open, for which I'm grateful. The ankle leash rips in two, falling away like a piece of scrap leather.

I grip my twin, whose chest is heaving with the relief of being unchained. "You're brilliant, Rafi. Absolutely perfect."

Rafael grips his sternum, and for the first time I notice a twist of pain on his face. "Ugh. You weren't kidding about that shock."

I envision a halo of light around Rafael's head. "You electrocuted yourself for my brother?"

"*Our* brother," Rafi corrects. "And of course I did."

I love him. There is nothing more to it than that. I love my brother for sacrificing himself so unselfishly. "Thank you."

Rafi's mind is more on task than mine, even as he flexes his jaw and shakes out the shock from his hand. His claws recede and the umber flesh returns. "Santiago, we need some way to knock out the other slaves. We can't have their Chupacabras attacking us when we make our escape. We might have a way to cure them when we get to the mainland, but even if we can't, they deserve to be rescued as much as we're able."

Santiago pieces together a plan quicker than I can keep up. "My healer bag is in the barn. I have enough bella donna in there to put them all to sleep. Quick!"

And just like that, Santiago is one with my other family. Two of my brothers run with me toward the barn, the night air reviving whatever hope I thought I'd lost to despair. It's so natural to run with my brothers, to dash into the night toward whatever catches our eye. My aching muscles suddenly feel freed with a fresh burst of life.

It's all I can do not to stare at Santiago instead of the path ahead of me, but miraculously, I manage to get to the barn without tripping over my own two feet.

Santiago holds up his hands to me. "Stay out here. If

any of the Chupacabras come out, it's going to be more danger than you can handle."

I quirk my brow at him.

Santiago loosens his shoulders with a chuckle. "Okay, fine. It's more than *I* can handle to see you hurt, which very well might happen if one of the Chupacabras comes out."

Rafael rests his hand on my shoulder. "We'll wait around the back. Don't dose them yet. We still have to get them to the boat. I don't feel like dragging them the whole way."

Santiago studies Rafi as he replies. "The bella donna takes several minutes to kick in, but it numbs their animal right away before it knocks the person out. It's a small window we'll have to get everyone to the boats, but it's manageable."

I can tell Rafi doesn't like the prospect of possibly having to haul several bodies to the shore, but as it's our only escape plan, it's time we take it.

Santiago holds my gaze, his lower lip quivering. I can tell he doesn't want to leave my presence.

I grip the back of his head in the same way Cruz always does to me, and press my forehead to my brother's. "I will be here when you get out. Now go, so I can take you home."

Santiago takes a step away but then stops. "The

Massacooramaan! Even if we get all the way to the boats, there is a man who lives in the sea. He guards the island and keeps us from escaping!"

I grin at my brother, feeling the slightest bit smug. "Took care of that already."

Rafi grins, just as cocky as I am. "Santos stabbed the Massacooramaan through his heart."

The look on Santiago's face is priceless, and fills me with a masculine pride that makes me feel like I could lift a truck. He gapes at me with reverence, like I'm a king or something.

When we part ways, I run with renewed vigor toward the volcano to alert Tio Bruno and Tavita. Though my body knows it should be shutting down after this much exertion, no food and little sleep, the prospect of the finish line brings me back to life.

I don't even realize until I look over my shoulder that Rafael isn't with me.

My stomach drops when Rafael shifts into his dragon, looming around Máximo's hut. His long, forked tongue flicks in and out, like he's hoping Máximo will realize something is amiss.

My feet carry me quickly to the volcano. I only hope we can escape this dreaded place before it's too late.

9

POETIC JUSTICE
RAFAEL

Even though there has been no sign of movement from inside the hut, my tail flicks like a cat toying with its prey. I haven't had enough time inside the fully-formed skin of my animal. I can get around well enough, but it's like driving a machine with no labels on the controls. I can figure out the basics, but I'm certain there is more I'm capable of that I just haven't figured out yet.

I could make myself useful helping the slaves to the dock. Santiago has his hands full, escorting and sometimes dragging the weighted bodies that are partway anesthetized to the shore. There are more than I realized. More than anyone hoped. There are two boats and ten captives, plus the four of us. It'll be tight, but we'll figure it out.

Those words have seen us through many a dust-up that went south. Santos, Cruz and I always keep the mindset that whatever the danger is that kicks us in the teeth, we'll figure it out. We're the best at fighting the Kalku in part because we have that certainty.

It's not dawn yet, but too near it for my liking. I can feel the birds and bugs waking up to announce the morning. I want to tell them all to hold off for another ten minutes. I can see Santos with Tio Bruno and Tavita in the distance, but they're not near enough for me to drop my posture of protection. I won't shift back until everyone is in the boats and we're well on our way.

No one else has shifted, thank goodness. I think any notion their Chupacabras had at making an appearance was stifled when they saw the girth of my dragon.

At least we don't have to worry about that.

It's a relief to see Santos running to his brother, helping him load the now unconscious slaves into the boats. They work well together, or maybe it's just that Santos works well enough with anyone who gives him half a chance.

Two of them. There will be two of them now. I will have three whole brothers to get into trouble with.

I cannot wait.

I'm not on my guard, too distracted by the sight of

them to see the flash of light before it knocks me in the face.

A hard whip cracks over the bridge of my long nose. Before I can register what it was or where it came from, there's already blood blooming across my face, cold and sticky as it trickles to the sand.

Pain so deep it scares me ricochets through my body, pushing a roar out of me that shakes the hut.

Tavita cries out, but I cannot think about anything but the red film that's now covering my vision.

I've never seen Máximo in real life. When he darts toward me from his hut, I'm a little disappointed at how short and squat the man is. How did he get so many to follow him? How did he inspire so much hate?

Adelita's words echo in my head even as I right myself and stomp toward him. "Evil only needs permission to thrive." That's what Máximo gave the twisted men who stole me from my parents. He gave them permission to act on their chilling urges.

They gave him permission to become a danger to anyone in his path.

And this morning as the sun finally peeks over the horizon, I give myself permission to end him once and for all. Santiago doesn't think Máximo can be killed, but he didn't know the Luz Mala has gone out. That's gotta count in my favor.

I'm not waiting around another few decades for time to end this madman. Máximo dies today.

Another roar belches out of me, only this time, it's with purpose and rage. When I step forward, it's like I'm pushing a button that unleashes a new level of danger. Heat ripples through me and aims itself like a hose straight at my prey.

Máximo's round face looks just as surprised as I am that a monster like me exists.

A monster like me. There's a cruel twist of fate for both of us. I'm addicted to milkshakes and still laugh at fart jokes. His people took me and made me into half a monster. Adelita finished the job with a kiss, and now the monster they tried to create is being unleashed on their founder, their leader...

...their scapegoat.

Máximo is the reason the Kalku do what they like.

And now he's the reason I'll do what *I* like.

Rage the likes of which I never tap into heats my bones until I'm certain my insides will turn molten. *I am the volcano now. I am the danger.*

Fire belts out of me and lights onto his hut. I was aiming for him, but burning his home up is a good second choice. He stole mine from me when I was a baby; this is poetic justice.

Máximo is livid, his features pinched as he shouts into the night, "Come, my soldiers! Take down this pest!"

I'm not sure if my dragon can smile, but I sure am grinning on the inside. His shifters are sedated, leaving him all by his lonesome. Big men with a plan are only as formidable as the followers they collect. *"Evil needs permission to thrive."* Without a crowd, all they have is useless bitterness being shouted into the void.

Máximo cries out at my dragon's fire. I can't aim it properly, but the effect is awe-inspiring enough to catch even me by surprise. I want to tear Máximo apart with my claws, but my arms are short, so a long-range attack seems the best bet, even if my aim is off.

I should have trained harder. I was afraid to let my dragon out because I didn't want to be even more ostracized in the village. But this is my own fault. I should have taken my strength more seriously. I didn't understand why Adelita shied away from her muscle until my dragon grew to be a force even I didn't want to reckon with.

Now that the showdown is here, all I have is fire.

All I have is rage.

Luckily, I've been suppressing that shit for decades, and it's been looking for a place to explode.

When Máximo calls for his Chupacabras again, I stomp toward him, my temper lost, along with my control. My dragon wants to bite his round head off, and I have no desire to hold my animal back. The roar that hits the air sends chills down my spine as I crash through the bramble toward the man whose wicked ambition ruined so many lives.

Just before my jaws clamp down, that whip made of light snaps across my snout again. My body rears, my head flying back as I howl a wounded roar into the dawn. I can't see; the pain is so great that I don't know which way to aim my fire. The whip wasn't anything Máximo was holding; it was a spell that manifested something sharp out of nothing and disappeared after it did its damage.

My vision isn't clear and neither is my head. It's all I can do to keep my upper half upright as I do what I can to stand my ground.

Another stripe of agony belts across me, this time hitting my chest. The heat vibrates through my body, and somehow, I know it has inflicted damage that cannot be undone.

My arms are sluggish now, my footsteps weighted as I try to make my way to Máximo. I was the predator, but by the smug gleam coming from the squat megalomaniac, we seem to have switched roles.

His whip did something to me. Aside from the excruciating pain, my limbs aren't working right anymore. In fact, when I try to take another step toward him, my foot won't lift.

My arms aren't moving, either.

Poison. There's a poison moving through me. I don't know how I can be so certain of this, but there's a burning sensation that doesn't just sizzle at the point of the whip, but it creeps inward, like so many tiny spiders scuttling through my veins.

Relief floods me when Tio Bruno's battle cry hits my ears. The man is a brute in every sense of the word, and that's exactly what I need on my side right now. How his body isn't out of commission from the decades of brutal force he's put himself through is beyond me. He runs like a man without limits, like he's never known any obstacle stupid enough to hold him back. I've never felt relief when I've seen Tio Bruno before, but it's the only thing that distracts me from the agony that's ripping through me and gaining momentum.

Tio Bruno doesn't bother with magic. He rushes Máximo with nothing but sheer will and a knife.

The flash of fear on Máximo's face is satisfying, to be sure, but short-lived. He touches Tio Bruno's forehead to push him away, but Tio Bruno's reaction isn't that of a man shoved. The military badass howls as if he's been burned. He falls back—a thing I never thought I would witness. He lands on his butt, holding his face as he shouts through whatever torture Máximo has inflicted.

Máximo stalks toward him, not even registering me as a threat. Of course, I can't move an inch, so I'm not actually anyone to be worrying about, apparently. The poison eats away at my muscle, feasting on my innards so quickly, my head spins. I want to break free and tear the head off this menace as he approaches Tio Bruno, but I can't move. All I can do is watch in horror as Máximo grins down at Tio Bruno, drawing his arm back to deliver what I can only guess will be a fatal blow.

I can't watch, and yet, my neck won't turn, so I physically cannot look away.

When a streak of movement rushes in my periphery, my heart soars. Santos is silent as he races toward the two. His fighting style is my favorite to watch.

Sometimes in brawls with the Kalku, I would get pummeled because I'd be distracted watching Santos at his finest. He is pure muscle and movement as he charges. Most would dart around Tio Bruno to get at Máximo, but Santos fights like a gymnast possessed. He runs straight at Tio Bruno from behind, leaps up and uses his shoulder as a jumping board. He's airborne, but doesn't use his arms to attack; instead he hurtles himself onto Máximo's shoulders, locking his knees on either side of the man's head.

His momentum carries him forward, which jerks Máximo back. Santos twists his lower half on the way down, throwing Máximo completely off his balance.

Máximo might have magic we've never mastered, but Santos has moves no one's ever been able to duplicate. His face is focused and serious, not a grunt or sound wasted.

When Máximo's laser whip comes at me again, he misses completely because Santos has him so out of sorts. He jerks the man's body around first with his legs and then with his arms, flipping Máximo so many times that I start to get motion sickness just by watching.

So transfixed am I that I don't notice Tavita until she's almost on top of the two. I want to roar for her to get back, but I can't move my mouth.

Máximo's whip lashes out at me again. I'm such a huge target that he can't possibly miss. This time, the edge of the whip pierces instead of lashes. Blood doesn't drip from my bulbous body, but splatters and flows without regard for sparing my life.

Fatal, my mind tells me—a fact from which I cannot inch away. The pain is still haunting me, but more loudly in my mind is the pronouncement that these are, in fact, my last moments.

Cruz isn't here. I always thought that when I did finally die, Cruz would be holding my hand.

Tavita's form catches my eye, distracting me from my agony. It's like they're putting on a play so I have something grand to go out to.

I don't know what I'm seeing until a few seconds after it's happened. Santos flips Máximo onto his back just long enough for Tavita to punch her fist to her father's sternum.

Only her fist doesn't stop at his flesh. I gasp—the shock outweighing the pain for the briefest of moments —as her arm sinks into his chest, penetrating through skin and bone. Her arm is buried past her wrist. Of all the things that have horrified me thus far, this one takes first place for most gruesome.

Máximo tenses, his back arching as a silent shriek freezes on his lips.

Tavita can walk through walls. She can walk through thick layers of rock to get into the heart of a volcano.

I guess she can reach through skin and bone, too.

Tavita screams—half horrified and half triumphant —as she rips her arm from Máximo's chest, holding in her hand something meaty and raw, dripping with blood.

She... Tavita...

She ripped his heart out of his chest. Pure wonder trumps the agony in my body for the briefest of seconds. I never would have predicted this being Máximo's end.

A daughter murdering her father using the genetic enhancements that came from him to end his life is a concept so grand, I can scarcely wrap my mind around it.

Maybe this is what people mean when they use the phrase "poetic justice."

Every stitch of pain leaves me in the next breath, deserting my body so completely that for a second, I question if it was ever really there.

My dragon deserts me, waving a quick "peace out" because this scene is too much for him. My claws recede and my body collapses onto the sand, taking the last of my fight away as the world tunnels and then fades from view.

Cruz isn't here. It's my last moment, and my brother isn't holding me.

I can hear Santos shouting my name, but I can't lift my head to get to him. Santos runs to me, my brother who has never let me fight my battles alone. He kneels in the pool of my dragon's blood, crying out as if my death might just be the thing that kills him. "No! No, Rafi! Look at my face. I can fix this! I'll fix this!"

But he can't, and we both know it. There's nowhere for him to place his hand because my entire torso has been flayed open. I can't lift my hand, but somehow Santos knows that I want to touch his cheek. He lifts my palm and presses it to the side of his terror-stricken face. "Brother," is all I can manage.

Santos shouts out a guttural sob that breaks what's left of my bleeding heart. "Brother!"

Adelita will be good to him. Cruz will look after him. Santiago will fill the missing piece that losing me will leave him with.

Máximo is dead.

If that's not a good note to go out on, I'm not sure I'll find a better one even I did manage to live fifty years more.

The pain recedes, and along with it, the fear of whatever comes next on the other side of this life.

My eyelids close as the sound of the sea lapping at the shore lulls me into the next life, carried there in the arms of my brother.

10

SALVADOR'S SECRET SIN

CRUZ

I've felt off since the sun rose, and it's not just because Salvador showed us the monarch of Anzaldúa lying in a medically-induced coma in a secret room in Salvador's home. Something's shifted in my sternum, making every position I take feel uncomfortable and wrong.

I scoot closer to Adelita on the hard couch across from the ruler's supine form, forgoing the demeanor I usually take when I'm interrogating someone. This unquantifiable unrest in my chest only eases up when part of me is touching Adelita. "Tell me again, Salvador. I want to understand, but it's looking bad from where I sit."

Salvador paces in the dank, mud-packed room that's lit by a single bare bulb. His father lies across from our sofa, making me wonder how many nights Salvador has foregone his own bed and slept here, near his dad. The ruler looks stern, even in sleep.

Salvador ruffles his dark hair, his eyes haunted and without their usual mischief. Even as he glances at my sister, whom he clearly fancies, there's no merriment anywhere on his features. "No one knows that my father is being held down like this. I did this. I'm the one who knocked him out and kept him under. It's not for the usual reasons you might be already concluding. Sure, I'm next to rule, but I didn't want to come into the position after all the damage he'd done to Anzaldúa. There's a reason it's considered abusive to sequester your people away from the outside world. If a man did that to his wife—forbade her to speak or go near anyone other than his approved people—that would be an obvious red flag. My father's been doing that to our people for decades. Ever since Máximo took power and the Kalku started gaining in their conquests, he prohibited anyone from going to the surface, except on extreme mission from him."

When Salvador keeps pacing and stops speaking, I fill in the gap. "He was scared, it sounds like."

Salvador points at me as his feet move. "That's what I thought at first. I thought he was being protective of us. But then people started disappearing."

Eva stiffens where she stands near the exit. "What do you mean?"

"Anyone who questioned him would mysteriously come down with some rare disease, which people started calling cocoliztli. Then they would die a few days later. Or their bodies would go missing, and they'd never be heard from again. Do you know how hard it is for someone to go missing in an underground civilization?" He taps on the wall, which, when I look closer, I can see is slightly different than the walls outside of this room. It's all packed dirt like the tunnels, but there are bits of rock sediment or something mixed in.

I swallow hard. "Sounds like you're saying he took matters into his own hands."

"I didn't want to believe it at first, but there wasn't much that could be argued that he didn't stamp out. So I went in search of the bodies that disappeared. I've found sixty-three so far, but I'm always searching for more." He runs his palm over the wall. "Father needed ultimate control, so much that when I spoke out, he put me on restrictions." Salvador pauses and swallows hard. "One day, my polenta didn't taste right. I made myself throw up because I knew he was onto me."

Adelita stands, migrating to his side. She can't help herself when someone is in pain. Compassion is engrained deep in her bones. "Which was worse—the poison, or the fact that you knew it was your father who'd done it?"

Salvador turns his chin to Addy, looking positively haunted. "Death is nothing to selfishness like that, but the poison was no picnic, either. I used to sing, you know."

Adelita's reply is soft. "I didn't know. Why did you stop?"

Salvador cups his throat. "My voice wasn't always raspy like this. The poison he used tore up a good part of me. I lived, but there's the constant reminder of his thumbprint every time I speak up for myself. Poetic, that bastard."

I don't know what to say to that. Don Luis is wicked, that's for sure.

Adelita sits on the side of Don Luis' bed, looking innocent next to the madman. I want to scoop her up and get her away from him, but her choices are her own, and I know controlling her movements is a bad idea.

Still, I itch to steer her away from the monster in man flesh.

"Tell me how you handled that," she says quietly, beckoning him to her.

Instead of sitting on the bed beside her, Salvador kneels before her, as if begging for absolution. I know that feeling well. Adelita holds serenity in her open palm. I often find myself begging for a fraction of that peace.

When Salvador doesn't answer, Adelita prods with a gentle, "When we're faced with adversity, we have two choices: to act or to accept. It sounds like you accepted quite a bit, but then ran out of patience. That's understandable. So you felt the need to act. Tell me about that."

Salvador's gravelly voice comes out quiet. Nothing in the room moves, and all eyes are on him. "I didn't have the gall to end my own father. When I tried, he laughed and called me weak, because I couldn't go through with it. So I waited until he slept and crept into his chambers. He's on a heavy dose of sedatives that keeps him in a constant coma. I should end him for all the lives he's taken, but I am not a killer. I can't go through with it." He stares lifelessly at Addy's knees. "I guess I am weak."

Adelita reaches for him and grabs onto his hands, tilting her head to the side once he finally looks up at her. "Do *you* think you are weak? Whose truth are you living by?"

Salvador swallows, pausing to process her words. "I think I am not my father, but there are pieces of him in me. When I found those bodies of the people who opposed him, I should have buried them in the mass grave we use for our people when they pass on. But I didn't. I spackled them into the walls of this room, so my father would be surrounded by his sins." He lowers his chin and shakes his head. "Who does that? I'm sick, just like he is."

Eva steps toward them. "I'll tell you what kind of person does that: a poet, that's who. You didn't murder those people. You wanted your father confronted with all he's done, so you trapped him in a room where he couldn't escape them. Even in death, their protests confront him. It's poetic, and nothing darker than that."

Her certainty leaves no room for argument.

Mierda. She called him a poet. It's the kind of man Eva's always fantasized about.

I guess I'm going to have to get used to Salvador.

The sediment in the walls isn't rock, but bone. I can't help my grimace, but I respect the thought that went into Salvador's actions.

"Why didn't you kill him?" Adelita inquires.

Salvador keeps his head bowed. "Because murder isn't in the job description of a leader. At no point will I tolerate my people following someone with patricidal blood on his hands. Anzaldúa deserves better than what they were given in my father. I cannot be better if I am the same. So I hid him away and spread the rumor that he's become a recluse in his advancing years. I've taken the past few months and let my people breathe. They can see the sun whenever they wish now. They're free. Of course, some are too afraid of fresh air, afraid of freedom. They don't want to be close to the sun. That's their choice, but the option is finally there for those who would seize it." He closes his eyes, squeezing Adelita's hands. "It's not the right path, I'm sure, but I don't know what is. We don't have a system for removing a faulty leader. My father rules until he dies."

Eva kneels beside him. "If you were to take charge of your people, tell me what that would look like."

Salvador sits back on his heels, dropping Addy's hands so he can gaze into my sister's countenance. "It would look much like it does now, I imagine, except that I would want to build aboveground, too. We don't need to hide as much as we need to stand our ground. I've studied your father's rule for many years. I cannot imagine I would do things much different than he's done for your people. Don José is a good man." His voice drops with the note of a vow to it. "I would allow my people to marry outside of our own tribe. We cannot thrive if the only ideas we're ever exposed to are our own. Perhaps that's the difference between my ideals and that of Cáceres. I do not wish to have a wall to keep those who need help locked out."

That seals it. I can almost see a physical tie linking the two of them together. Salvador honoring Dad and wanting to marry outside his tribe is just as good as a love poem in Eva's eyes.

I avert my eyes when my sister kisses Salvador, but I can still hear the sound of their lips coming together. Truthfully, it's the sound of two tribes coming together, despite what any wall would dictate. Above the ick factor that is my sister in any romantic setting, the cementing of an ally is nothing to sneeze at.

I stand the second they break apart. "Eva, take Salvador back into the living room. Take him for a walk. Take him anywhere but here."

Eva stands, her eyes wet. She doesn't ask me what I'm going to do; she knows. The only reason I said yes to coming here was based on the olive branch that had been offered by Anzaldúa, letting us hide Adelita here. The fact that it was Salvador all along seeking out peace and not his father?

I know what Cáceres needs me to do.

Eva wraps me in a firm hug. "Thank you, Cruz. You have always been a leader."

I don't want her hug to soften me, but it always does. That's probably why I didn't let her near me for so many years. I was afraid the softening would make me less of a hero, but that's never been true. My family's love strengthens me whenever I can learn to let it.

I keep one arm around my sister and reach down to

help Salvador to his feet. I shake his hand with the firmness of a promise. "We want to unite with your tribe and help you acclimate to the world. If I can help enforce your rule, I will." My chest barrels. "Cáceres will help Anzaldúa see the sun however we can."

Salvador is bent on making me uncomfortable, it seems, because he foregoes the handshake and hugs me. "I am grateful for you, Brother."

Jeez, this guy.

I slide both of them off of me and coax them toward the door. "Yeah, yeah. Out you go. Hammer out the details in the living room while I do my job in here." When they leave hand-in-hand, I meet Adelita's eyes and jerk my head to the exit. "You too, Addy."

She tilts her head to the side, looking up at me with a scrutinizing eye. "You really thought that would work on me?"

I exhale a short laugh. "You don't want to be here for this."

"I want to be here for *you*. Don't you get that? You're busy taking out everyone else's trash, but who helps you with yours?"

I run my hand over my face. "This isn't what I want you to be part of, baby. You're a good person. Snuffing out a sleeping old man? That's beneath you."

Adelita stands, enveloping herself in my arms. A

portion of my tension leaves at her close proximity. I didn't realize it, but I need her near me in moments like this. I crave any kind of softness that keeps my soul from icing over.

Her voice is quiet, disturbing the silence. "Where you go, I go," she vows. "Pillow?"

I hate this. I mean, as far as enemies go, killing one of them without bloodshed and without a fight is really preferable to the usual bloodbath. But as I pick up the pillow and press it over the man's face, I worry too much of my soul might have been chipped away throughout my life by moments exactly like this.

I don't want Adelita to see this part of me, but when she touches my back as I suffocate the old man, I'm surprised to find I'm grateful I'm not alone. She doesn't leave me, even when I'm certain I am at my worst.

My imagination goes into overdrive, and for a moment, I envision the bodies that have been spackled into the walls migrating out to watch their murderer's death. There's tension in the air that isn't coming just from me, and though I know I'm being superstitious, I feel them watching me from the beyond.

They have been waiting to be avenged.

I shouldn't let this affect me. Everyone knows what a terrible dictator Don Luis has always been. But this conquest is wrapped in significance that will change two entire tribes. My actions always have consequences, but this one will change the future of both Anzaldúa and Cáceres to a track I cannot predict.

It takes one minute for the man to die, but ten before I pull the pillow away, just to be certain.

The fluffy thing is weighted in my hands like a boulder I might always have to carry. When it falls to the floor, my entire body is heavy with purpose. It's never mattered that I am the one with blood dripping off my hands. Rafi and Santos have the same grim purpose. It's how we serve Cáceres. Our dirty hands ensure everyone else's can stay clean. There are people in the army who have never murdered a man before, and that's the way I like it.

And just like that, the specters that haunt this room lose their tether to this world. I can feel them leave, knowing they have been vindicated.

But I've felt off since the sun rose. Even after the incredible night I shared with Adelita, I can't erase the unrest that plagues me. Now that I've ended a monarch, my bones ache like they are certain they will never know peace.

Adelita catches me when my feet stumble back. She lowers me to the couch, and because I trust her, I let my body go where she directs. "I'm here," she promises. "I'm right here."

"Something's wrong!" Even though we're alone, I whisper my worry. "Not with this," I clarify, motioning to the dead man on the bed. "Something else. I don't know what. I feel off." I close my eyes and shake my head, disgusted that I sound so emotive and strange. "I can't think of the right words. I don't know what my deal is."

Adelita sits beside me, smoothing her hand over my chest.

Her eyes are wet, too good and pure to have witnessed the man's murder, no doubt. Still, she's by my side, braving my darkness so I don't have to wallow through the muck alone. "You carry so much on your shoulders, Cruz. It's okay to call a spade a spade and admit the load is heavy."

My entire body sags because she says the exact right thing. She gives me a safe place, so for once in my life, I take what I want. "I don't want to travel so much anymore," I admit, grimacing at the scandal. "I know I said so before, but I meant it. I want to put down roots. I want to get to know my people."

When Adelita cuddles into my chest, the knot tied too tight behind my sternum finally begins to loosen. "We all support you in that, Cruz."

"I know. I think I just needed to hear it again. It's a big change."

When I swing my chin down to catch her lips in a kiss, I intend for a quick connection to brighten up a second or two of our lives. But what greets me turns into several minutes of slow, heart-drenched kisses that tangle us together even more than we already are. Her compassion accepts me for the broken man I am, and her strength reminds me that I cannot remain this way. I do the dirty work, sure, but I am not allowed to do it alone anymore. There will be no more excuses for me hiding away so the bitterness can fester.

My source of light will find me and kiss the life back into my cold and weary bones.

"I love you," I admit when our lips finally part, my forehead soldered to hers.

Her eyes burn with a boldness I pray will never be stamped out. "I love you too much to ever let you go through something like this by yourself. So the next time you think about sending me away, don't bother. *You* are my business. Your pain is mine, so don't be selfish with it."

I can only hope our future is paved with happiness, but the ominous dread in my gut tells me something grim still awaits.

11

RAFAEL'S BROTHER
SANTOS

No one here except for Tio Bruno knows sign language, not even Santiago. It's the only language I can speak now, and I'm grateful they don't understand me. Tio Bruno only knows the bare minimum for basic communication—nothing like the incoherent storm that's grown too loud in my head.

I don't want them to know the chaos raging in my soul. I don't want them to know me at all. The boat ride was long, especially since I didn't help with the rowing. Santiago rowed our boat by himself. Tavita and Tio Bruno rowed the other with the slumbering shifter slaves sprawled all over each other.

They tried to get me to put down Rafael's body, but apparently, nobody knows me because if they did, they never would have asked me something so unforgiveable.

Tio Bruno fetched a blanket from Máximo's hut and wrapped Rafi's split-open body up because when I lifted him off the sand, his carcass nearly severed into two pieces. It wasn't just the whip of light that tore him up, but some sort of poison that ate away at his insides, softening his bones and making them too weak for much movement.

Still, Rafael will not be buried on some awful island away from us, his family. Also, part of me knows Cruz will not believe it unless he sees the proof.

But even if those other reasons did not exist, I still would not be able to part from my brother. Rafael is mine, and I will protect him as such.

I can see the shore, but nothing in me lifts. I'm tired and hungry, yet I know if food was presented, I couldn't eat a bite.

Rafi, Rafi, Rafi...

My heart is on a constant loop of mourning. Even when the ship docks on the mainland, there is nothing on my mind but him.

Tio Bruno made sure we didn't go to the harbor nearest the island, in case more Kalku had congregated, waiting to take us out. It was a longer boat trip, but the normalcy that greets us when we dock is worth it. My commander trots to a man nearby who is working on his boat and asks to use his phone.

Help will be on the way soon.

None of it matters. Rafael is me. I am him. He survived the Kalku as I did. No matter how strange my actions were when I was first liberated, Rafi stayed with me, fighting through the noise in my head over losing Santiago so I wouldn't be alone in my new life.

And now Rafael is alone in his new life, drifting from this one into the next without me. What if they don't smile at his jokes? What if no one gets his sense of humor? What if they don't take care of him? What if his dragon isn't accepted?

Or worse yet, what if there is no afterlife, and Rafi's essence just ceases to exist?

No. I don't believe that. Rafi's life was too potent and pure to simply evaporate into nothingness.

I clutch him closer, kissing his forehead that has long turned waxy with tints of greenish gray around the edges.

I don't care. He stayed with me when I was Santos the Savage. He made me into a person. I can do the same for his broken body until Cruz and I can properly bury our brother.

Santiago has been respectful of my agony, speaking very little on the way over. But when Tio Bruno comes over and reaches down to take Rafi, Santiago speaks up. "No. Santos needs this man."

"He's exhausted," Tio Bruno counters, not unkindly. "He's in shock, too. None of us have eaten or slept in a long time." His large hand weights my shoulder. "Let me take him, Santos."

I clutch Rafi tighter, barring my teeth to let Tio Bruno know that I am not reformed one bit. I am still the savage I've always been. I will not hold back now if my family is taken away from me.

Tio Bruno steps back, his hand running over his face. "Alright, then. I'll get us some food. A few of the soldiers will be by to get us in a couple hours." To Santiago, he explains. "It's a long trek to our village. They're coming as fast as traffic permits. You'll come with us, all of you. Cáceres is safe." Then, with compassion I didn't realize Tio Bruno had in him, he says, "You are safe now."

Santiago lowers his head, tears dripping down his cheeks. "Thank you, Sir."

"Tio Bruno," he corrects. "I'm Santos' uncle. Since he's your brother, that means I'm *your* uncle, too."

Confusion sweeps over me. Sure, I claim him as my uncle because that's what I'm supposed to do, but he's never claimed me as his family before. I glance up at him, truly perplexed.

Tio Bruno looks down at me with a hardness in his eyes that tells me he means business. "Look at me, Son.

There is nothing you could have done to safe Rafael. I saw the whole thing. We barely got out of there alive. If not for Tavita experimenting with her own magic on the fly, we all would have died. You did everything you possibly could, and Rafael died in the arms of someone who truly loves him. At the end of the day, not many of us will be held so nobly when we pass on." Tio Bruno nods once, his stern features eliminating the notion of an argument. "You can hold Rafael as long as you need, Santos. When you're ready, I will help you bury him."

I don't know what to say to any of that, so I simply hold Rafi tighter, clutching him to my chest because that's where he belongs.

They tell me it's been hours when the soldiers finally come to take us home, but I don't notice the time. I don't notice much of anything, except when one of the soldiers tries to remove Rafi from my grip. My arms are weak and trembling, but they still have some fight left in them. Luckily, Tio Bruno comes to my aid, backing the helpful soldier away so no one takes Rafael from me.

I carry my brother with quaking arms into the back of the car, cradling him across my lap. Santiago sits beside me in the back after the cadejo slaves have been dosed with a second round of a sedative to ensure we make it back to the village without incident.

Water and food are passed around, but I turn my

head from all of it. I can't let go of Rafi. We are two cave slaves who had to learn how to survive in a world that was too civilized for us.

The others ignore me as they usually do, but Santiago's arm finds its way around my shoulders. While I hold Rafi, my brother holds me. So deep is my devastation that I can't fully press into the relief I feel at having Santiago with me again.

Santiago's voice is quiet as he hums a low lullaby to me, soothing the parts of me that might never stop aching completely. The entire ride back to the village, Santiago acts as my sentry, speaking for me when words are too difficult to utter.

It's evening when we reach the village. Somewhere along the lines I am told that Cruz and Adelita are on their way home, now that Máximo is confirmed to be dead.

Heartless, I want to tell them, not dead. The Luz Mala went out, but the emeralds are still intact. We need to destroy them. Until we do, Máximo is not dead. Even with his heart ripped out, I am certain of this one thing.

Everyone else is content to believe the big, bad boogeyman is dead. I'm too lost to correct them.

Though I've reached a level of exhaustion I didn't realize existed, I carry Rafael to his bedroom, ignoring Consuela's shrieks as I finally lay Rafi out across the sheets. Even with my most active imagination, I cannot tell myself he's merely sleeping. His face is gray now, but most telling of all is that the light which usually dances in my brother's eyes has left this world completely, and I feel gone along with it.

There is no Rafi without his jokes.

I recline beside him, pretending we're resting in between one of our many treks to fight the Kalku. Before Adelita, Cruz, Rafi and I shared a mattress most of the time.

His weight is all off—too light on his side. I don't feel him beside me, even though his pallid form is there, staring unblinkingly at me.

When Dad comes into the room however long later, he's accompanied by Tio Bruno. He wears a grim mask of sadness to hide the disgust beneath. Apparently lying in bed with my dead brother is frowned upon.

I could not care less.

Dad brings a chair to my side and sits down, leaning forward with his elbows on his thighs and exhaling heavily. "I'd like to know what happened, Son. Can you walk me through it?"

When I turn my head, I can see his eyes are wet. Rafi is his family, too, no matter how oddly the two of us fit into this home.

I sit up and turn, foregoing sanity because I'm hours

past that. My arms find their way around my dad's neck, unlocking guttural sobs from the rock of a man. He's always had a heart of pure kittens and smiles, and now his son is dead decades before his time.

My dad's tears finally set my own loose, and they flow over his shoulder while we mourn together. We hold each other together while we fall apart, creating a safe place for such things like irreparable grief.

"I love you," Dad tells me through his tears. "Do you know that? Do I tell you that enough to where it sticks? Because I do, Santos. You are my son, and I'm sorry for anything that's ever taken you away from me. You've belonged under my roof from birth. I know it in my heart that you are mine." His body shudders over and over. "Rafi is my boy, too."

He's known me only two years, but Rafi has been with Don José from the age of five.

"He was so scared when he came to live with me, but he never showed it. He used to make up plays and dance to make me laugh. He had this song about farts that... well, is entirely inappropriate right now, but I keep singing it over in my head." Dad sobs on my shoulder, losing any semblance of composure. "When I would tuck the boys in at night when they were little, I would tell them I loved them with all my heart, and Rafi would say he loved me with all his farts." He laughs through his grief. "I love that little goofball, and I'm so proud of the man he became. Did I tell him that? Did he know he was mine?"

I nod, but I'm still not ready to speak. Instead, I pull back and sign as much. *"Rafi adores you. There is no question in his mind that you are his father. He's been well-loved ever since he moved in here, as have I."*

Don José chokes through his tears, scrubbing them over his red face. "I love you, Santos. You are my boy, and I'm so proud of the man you've become. And you bring me home another son on the day I've lost one of my babies?" He shakes his head. "You are always the thing my heart needs, Santos. Never forget that."

I hiccup through a few more sobs, nodding to let him know that I've finally heard him. After two years of him constantly telling me that I am loved and that I belong, it finally sinks in. I hear his tears and see his heart more clearly than I've ever understood this great man before. He loves without limits, which is too grand for my mind to grapple with most days.

His hand cups my shoulder so he can look me in the eye. "We have to take Rafael outside now, Santos. I need you to let us take him. It won't be any other soldiers, only Bruno and me. We'll be careful with his body."

It's one leap too many. I shake my head and lay back

down, this time wrapping my arms around Rafi's broken body so no one can take him from me.

Tio Bruno sighs from his spot in the corner, but it's not from frustration. His face is filled with distress as he motions to us on the bed. "I've seen many soldiers die over the years, even held a few while they passed, but I've never loved any of them like this. Take all the time you need, Santos. Come, José. Your son just died. You don't need to see this. I'll stay with them."

I've never really appreciated Tio Bruno properly, but when he escorts Don José out of the bedroom to shield him from the grotesque sight of his son cuddling up to the dead body of his other son, I appreciate him anew. Just because his heart beats beneath armor doesn't mean it is not there.

Tio Bruno sits in the chair by the bedside, saying nothing as I hold Rafi tight. I trust that even as I drift off in fits and spurts, he won't let anyone take Rafi away from me.

I don't know what time it is or what day when Cruz comes into the bedroom. He's been adequately prepared, but Rafi's body is in a state of atrophy that many cannot stomach. The smell of rot has long since permeated my nose, but still I cannot let him go.

Cruz climbs in on Rafi's other side, kissing his forehead as fresh tears splash down on the corpse. It's not my brother anymore, I have to admit. I'm holding tight to a carcass. Yet I cannot let go. My arms are frozen in place and my body too stiff to grant Rafi his release.

"Goodnight, brother," Cruz rasps. "You lived well. It's time you rest well, too." Then Cruz leans down and slides his arms beneath the blanket that covers Rafi's body.

Terror revives my senses that haven't known food or drink in too many days. "No!" I finally say aloud. "You can't take him away!"

I know my protest wounds Cruz, but he's gentle with my fragile state. "Help me, then. Let's take him outside together. Dad shouldn't have to see this."

Cruz can talk me into just about anything. I trust him above all else, so when he asks for my help, I give him whatever he needs.

My body is stiff and weak, but I manage to stand. Cruz does the heavy lifting, and I prop Rafael's head so it doesn't break off. "His bones are brittle. Careful," I caution as we make our way through the house and out into the sun.

The brightness of the day mocks me, so I scowl away from it. Nothing should be cheerful today, not even nature. There's a stretcher with one of the women from the village standing beside it, her head bowed. "I am so sorry, Santos," she says with the utmost respect for my pain.

Respect is a strange thing, I guess, but losing someone we love is a tragedy that unites even the savages among us.

I nod to the woman as we lay Rafi out on the stretcher. Cruz is abrupt in his speech, telling her exactly how Rafi is to be buried. He is to be given the burial of an heir to the throne, no matter that he's not blood. His body will be lain to rest in the tomb of Cruz's ancestors, and Rafael is to be dressed in his military threads.

The sight of Adelita catches me off-guard, making my tired heart stutter and skip several important beats. Her face is tear-streaked as she approaches the stretcher. There are no children playing nearby. No one is bustling about or talking above a whisper. One of their greatest protectors is now dead.

Adelita leans in and brushes Rafi's curly hair back from his face. Her voice is choked, but I can hear her lullaby clearly.

"*Sleep, baby, sleep.*
Dream, baby, dream.
Love, baby, love.

My baby, mine."

THEN ADELITA NODS to the woman in charge of the stretcher, and Rafael is wheeled away.

The moment my brother leaves my view, my legs give out, and my body plummets to the dirt.

12

SHOWERING SANTOS
ADELITA

Cruz won't let anyone pick up Santos, even though two men rush to help him when he collapses. Though Santos is no small child, Cruz is strong enough to make the effort of carrying him back inside look like it costs him nothing.

Tio Bruno meets us at the front door, holding it open for us as we hide away from the outside world. "Santos hasn't eaten or drank a thing in days. He's overly exhausted and needs looking after."

"Adelita and I have it from here." Cruz carries Santos to the bedroom the three of us share and lays him atop the mattress.

I can't see Santos like this. I can't watch Cruz stuffing down his grief because the situation needs taking care of, and he's always the one the crap falls on. I can't see Rafael laid out like he was. I can't see any of it, so I spin on my heel and beeline for the kitchen to hide out with Chef Aarón.

Aarón is crying over a bowl of pinto beans and onions, stirring without seeing what he's looking at.

I don't say his name or ask how he's doing. I set his spoon aside and wrap the old man in a hug. Aarón's tears turn audible as they streak onto my shoulder. "He was too young to die. Too happy to stop smiling. What will there be to smile about now? What hope is there without laughter? What is the point of any of this?"

His words make my insides tremble because there is no good answer. Before the guys found me and took me in, my closest friend was my mother, and I'd been without her for two years. Rafael was the smile that never took Cruz's temper too seriously. He could draw Santos out of the shell he so often wanted to hide inside.

Rafael kissed me without agenda and stayed with me when life proved too confusing to meander through on my own.

I wonder what the flavor was of his last milkshake.

I stay with Aarón, helping him make a meal for Santos, but I don't get more than five minutes in before Chef Aarón shoos me out with a glass of water to take to him. "Santos won't eat or drink anything. But if *you* tell him to drink the water, he will do it."

Of all the things to use my Ciguapa powers for, I guess keeping my guys alive is the best choice.

I feel like a little girl entering a room of adults when I make my way back into our bedroom. Don José is speaking with Cruz, the two of them conversing in hushed tones as more details are filled in on both sides. Eva stayed with Salvador to help him bury his father, Don Luis, and act as a show of support from our tribe to his.

Really, I know she doesn't want to face Rafael's death. I don't blame her. If I had a valid reason for being out of the area, I would be tempted to take it. I'd give anything not to have seen Rafael without the light in his eyes.

Santos is awake now, but he's not interacting. He stares lifelessly at the ceiling, his lips parted as if caught mid-confusion.

I set the glass of water on the nightstand and rummage through the drawer for pajamas and fresh underwear for Santos and for me. I move into the en suite bathroom, setting the clothes on the counter and getting everything ready because like it or not, Santos is taking a shower. He's stained with Rafael's blood and he stinks like death. I don't know what the right thing to do in this situation might be, but I know it can't start until Santos has the gore scrubbed off his body.

"Don't mind me," I say when I emerge from the bathroom and father and son both pause to regard me. "I'm going to wash up, and Santos is coming with me."

Santos blinks, which I take as a good sign.

I place my hand on Don José's arm. "Dad, would you mind getting some fresh sheets for the bed?" The ones I'm staring at have blood and body fluids leaked all over them.

Don José straightens, as if relieved to be given a job that might help his children. "Right away, *hija*." Then he kisses Cruz's cheek and squeezes Santos' toe before leaving us in the room.

I meet Cruz's eyes, seeing the hollow devastation that echoes my own. "Why don't you go help Chef Aarón with dinner. I'll get Santos cleaned up."

Cruz kisses my forehead, pressing part of his agony into my skin. "Do you need help with him?"

"I don't think so. You've been helpful enough for one day. Let Aarón overfeed you."

The corner of Cruz's mouth draws up, but he doesn't give birth to a full smile. I wonder when it will happen that any of us finds cause to laugh again.

Santos' chin turns to me when Cruz exits, but he doesn't speak. I'm not sure he has language right now. I know in times of distress, words desert him. It's probably best. Anything I can think of to say sounds asinine right now.

I can't do more than help him sit upright against the headboard and snuggle beside him on the bed. "I need you to drink a few sips of water, Santos. I know you don't want to, but it's important you do."

I know it's only because I ask that he entertains the cup when I press it to his lips. The few swallows are a small victory, but I'll take what I can get.

He has blood all over him—front and back. He hasn't changed his clothes in who knows how long.

"Come with me," I whisper, setting the cup down and helping him to his feet. He's weak and wobbly, but he doesn't fall on the way to the bathroom. With my arm to lean on, he stumbles only once. I manage to right him before he can fall completely, and somehow, we make it to the bathroom without him falling and without a protest. I lean him against the shut door and turn on the shower, testing the heat to make sure it doesn't cause him the least bit of discomfort.

I'm careful as I take off his clothing, giving him ample chance to stop me as I peel the jeans from his legs. My thumbs hook in the band of his underwear, but my eyes stay on his face even as I slide them over his toned legs. The soiled clothing won't be washed. I check his pockets and then put the clothes in the garbage bin, never to be worn again.

My clothes hit the floor next, distracting Santos enough to give a sliver of light to his eyes. The intrigue draws him closer, allowing me to lead him into the shower. It's not the way I would have hoped I would see Santos naked for the first time, but I will never tire of being the woman he needs in times of calm and in times of crisis.

I take my time soaping his body, paying special attention to the hard-to-reach places. The suds rise up on the chiseled planes, giving my hands the treat of a lifetime as they roam over a musculature that's hard to match. He earned each toned ripple the hard way, and each battle was well-fought.

There will be no comfort for Santos or Cruz, not for a very long time. Still, I can take care of them as they've looked after me when I didn't have all the answers.

I can tell Santos is torn by the sight of my nude body. The desire hooding his eyelids tells me he wants to make good use of our alone time, but the mourning throughout his being tells me this is the wrong moment to do so.

I make the choice for us both and continue washing him, pausing only for the sweetest of kisses to remind him that we are still here, and there's nothing we can't wade through together.

His body is a treat to wash. I love the way my hands slip over him. I can see a new facet of him this way, and I've come to learn that there is no part of Santos I do not love.

When I stand to wash his chest, Santos melts against my body, giving up the veil he has kept in place to ensure nothing hits him too hard. He trusts me with his raw, unpolished parts, so I vow my most sacred promise to be gentle with them.

My strength has always been tied to my gentleness, and right now, that is the superpower I call upon in our time of need. There is strength in my fist and also in my caress, and both serve me well when I learn which one should be accessed.

Santos' body is slippery and warm against mine, heated by the spray that pelts against his nape. His arms are finally responsive as they wrap around me. He holds me as if he is just now realizing I'm here.

"I will always come for you," I promise him. "No matter how lost you might be."

Santos tilts my chin up so he can kiss me—soft and sweet. He's still not ready to speak, which isn't something I'm about to push. I will be here when he's ready, and I will hold his hand when he's not.

I comfort Santos with my body, and he takes as much as he needs, following me as I lead him back to himself.

13

SUGAR THAT CURES SADNESS
ADELITA

The burial of Rafael was respectful and somber. Apart from the fact that Rafael would have hated it because, well, it's his funeral, I'm certain he would have loathed all the standing around in black with no stupid jokes whatsoever.

Rafi would not have hesitated to sweep me up in a quick dance—music or not. I am wearing a long black dress with capped sleeves and ruffles that brush my toes. No way would Rafi let that go to waste. He would insist this dress was made for dancing.

But in fact, it was made for mourning.

At the wake, I made myself useful looking after the kids so Consuela and Don José could grieve properly without parental distraction. I think the kids knew my heart wasn't into the sock puppet play I attempted, so we switched to my usual therapist routine, where I brought out crayons and paper so they could draw pictures of Rafael.

Most heart wrenching of all was Roberto's sketch, which featured Rafael in a green racing car with lightning shooting out the back. Roberto drew him as a superhero, which couldn't be more accurate than a still-life oil painting of the man.

None of us spoke much that night. It was a long evening of the usual "I'm so sorry for your loss," that when heard over and over gives a person the vitriolic and unreasonable urge to spout back a calloused, "Screw you," after the first hundred condolences.

That's when I knew I needed to take a break.

With the town square being littered with people, I excused myself and went back to the house. Though Cruz and Santos are aware of my every move, I'm glad they stayed in place when I told them I just needed some air.

Memories of my own mother's death are starting to come back, and I don't want to visit that place in my mind.

My footsteps carry me quickly away from the scene of mourners—many of whom wouldn't deign to look Rafael in the eye when he was alive, due to his childhood years spent in captivity with the Kalku. Now they're mourning his death, after spending the last two decades avoiding his life.

Give me a break.

My aim is to get inside the house and hide out under the guise of helping Chef Aarón in the kitchen or something. That's believable.

The fragrant scents of marinating goat and cilantro hit my nose before I step into the kitchen, but the second my foot enters Chef Aarón's domain, I hop back out when I spot the company. I was expecting Aarón's calming presence, not a second person whom I've been skillfully attempting to avoid.

"Oh! Sorry. I was just... You look like you've got everything covered in here." I turn awkwardly, but cringe when Aarón's voice stops my exit.

"Actually, would you mind helping me in here for a minute?"

My eyes close, but open again with a cheery smile by the time I turn back around to face them. "Of course. What do you need me to take out there?" I hope that by offering to bring food out of the kitchen, it will get me away from Santiago's gaze.

"Oh, this food is for the family, not the mourners. This stew needs to be stirred constantly, or it'll scald. Can you do that?"

It's as if Chef Aarón knows of my discomfort and is

purposefully trying to push me headfirst into the deep end to cure my aversion to it. I don't want to meet Santos' brother for real. I don't want him to see that I've accidentally hooked his brother and Cruz with my Ciguapa mojo. Santiago will hate me for luring in his brother like that. And what if he disapproves of me? Santiago and Cruz are the two people Santos reveres, and whose opinion of me truly matters to his own. Santiago won't like my blue eyes. He won't like that I'm Máximo's daughter, tainted in an irreparable way. Plus, I'm awkward and haven't truly learned how to fight properly. I have my strength, sure, but I can still be bested. How can he trust me to take care of Santos when the Kalku come to attack again, as they always do? I don't understand the Kalku culture. I made Santos get his photograph taken without knowing all the ins and outs of what that would do to his psyche. I'm learning, but I've got a long way to go before I truly understand all he's been through.

But when Aarón asks a favor of me, I don't have it in my heart to say no. He asks so little of anyone. "Sure, Aarón."

I pick up the long wooden spoon and stir slowly, making sure to scrape off any chunks that are trying to mold to the bottom of the pot.

I can feel Santiago's eyes on me, so I keep my gaze on the contents of the pot.

Aarón wipes his hands off on a dishtowel he has slung over his shoulder. "How is Santos today, *m'hija*?"

I really don't want to talk about Santos in front of Santiago. I'm not the authority on his own brother. "I'm not sure," I admit, which makes me feel even lower. I should know how my own boyfriend is doing on the day his family member is being put into the ground. "He's out there in a suit, nodding and being present, but he still isn't speaking. I don't want to rush that, but it's an indicator that he's not ready to share himself with the world yet. So we aren't pushing him." I stir slowly, though I can still feel Santiago's eyes burning a hole through the side of my face. "Maybe I should push him. I don't know what the right call is, only that Santos is not to be left alone. He's eating and sleeping, which is more than he was doing a few days ago."

Aarón pauses for a moment, and then pushes forward. "Santiago was wondering what his brother likes to eat now. I've shown him a few recipes, but honestly, Santos doesn't voice an opinion one way or the other. I can only go by the times he cleans his plate and stares at the platter because he's afraid to ask for seconds."

"You're a good man, Aarón. I love that you look for ways to know him better."

Aarón catches my eye with a tender smile. "Of course. When Santos first came into the house, he spent much of his time in the kitchen with me. Santiago is much the same so far. I rather enjoy the company. The people who come into the house from outside Cáceres become mine, learning how to take steps toward independence beside me." He picks up a spatula and flips the contents of the pan on the stove. "I never had children of my own, so Don José's family has been mine for as long as I've worked for the family." He points his spatula at Santiago, who is hovering in the corner, kneading bread. "Santiago is my new son. Never thought I'd be lucky enough to have twins, but I guess some people have light that constantly shines on them." He grins, and I love him for it. "My children learn to talk in here. They learn how to speak up for themselves and form opinions." His eyes flit to mine. "You are no exception, my dear."

I know he's waiting for me to speak my own, so I swallow hard and finally open my mouth. "I'm worried I don't know what I'm doing, Aarón. I'm a therapist, so I should know how to handle these situations. But this is a whole new ballgame."

Aarón kisses my temple. "There. Was that so hard?"

"Yes," I chuckle. But my smile dies because I know there is more I'm holding back.

Aarón looks over my shoulder and nods to Santiago, whom I can tell is biting his tongue against talking. "No one will be angry with you for speaking your mind, Son. What do you want to say?"

I turn to Santiago, bracing myself for the worst. I take a step back, panic clear in my face.

This is it. He's going to tell me what I already know: I am not worthy of Santos.

Santiago is dressed in jeans and a red polo, looking like Santos, but with a curiosity in his golden eyes that Santos holds tighter to the vest. "I don't know what my brother eats," he admits. In his slumped shoulders, I notice the same shame radiating from him that I see in myself. "He's my twin, and I don't know the details anymore."

Aarón's smile is filled with compassion, pleased that he constructed this moment of pure vulnerability for the two of us. "Santos eats what I serve the family for their meals, but he's never voiced a preference to me. I think I should like to put my foot down about that with you, Santiago. If you don't like something, it's okay to tell me."

Fear flares in Santiago's eyes as he takes a step back. "No, no. I'm grateful to be fed."

Aarón's smile falters. "I know you are, Son. This will all take some getting used to for you."

A silly idea dances in my mind. "Santos eats sugar now." This earns another look of shock from Santiago. "Since he's having a rough day, I was thinking of going out and getting him a special treat." I steel myself, braving a connection with this man who should loathe me. "Maybe you'd like to come with me?"

Caution is clear in Santiago's countenance. "It would make Santos happy?"

"I think happiness is a long way off right now, but it would bring him a small bit of comfort."

Santiago nods firmly. "Then I should very much like to go with you. Whatever might help Santos, I'll fetch it. Sugar really cures sadness?"

It's the cutest thing I've heard in a long time. "It's a start." Then to Aarón, I ask, "Is it okay if I take one of the cars?"

"Absolutely. Take whatever you want. Buy whatever you like. Just have fun." Aarón grins from ear to ear, pleased that we're building a bridge to somewhere in between our comfort zones.

Poor Santiago. I'm not sure he's ever known a comfort zone—only varying levels of fear.

"Thanks. I'm going to get changed first." I motion to

my elaborate black dress. If the Kalku happen upon us out there, this outfit won't do me any favors.

Aarón follows us out of the kitchen, instructing Santiago in hushed tones that shoes must be worn outside the house, and not to worry, he will help Santiago tie them.

My steps slow as I process the long road ahead for Santiago. Has he not worn proper shoes before? I try to remember what he wore when he came to me on the bus two years ago, and I think even in a bus crash, he had slip-on sandals.

He doesn't know how to tie his own shoes.

Compassion wells up in me. As I dress in black slacks and a matching sleeveless fitted magenta blouse, I remind myself not to take anything for granted. He's not accustomed to riding in a car, so freeways are probably a bad idea, due to the high speed limit. Will he get nervous in crowds? We'll do a drive-through, then. He hasn't been hugged by anyone other than his brother and maybe Tavita in who knows how long.

He drinks broth made with the hearts of women.

I cringe at the thought and at myself. It was not his doing. He was raised in a culture that makes little sense to me, and now he's been thrown into a new world that no doubt makes little sense to him.

Eva braided my hair this morning—several braids

that twist into a bun atop my head. I love the intricate style. With a little eyeliner she gave me, it makes my eyes stand out and my facial features more prominent.

When I step out into the hallway, Santiago has his hands tucked behind his back, like a soldier readying for orders. My mouth draws to the side as I debate how best to go about bonding with my boyfriend's brother—if such a thing is even possible.

"Thanks for coming with me," I say as I lead the way down the hall toward the back door. I'm so awkward with him, nervous and wanting him to like me, yet certain he won't. So I hedge my smile and keep a noticeable distance between my body and his.

"Of course." Santiago opens the door for me while I snake the keys off the hook near the exit. I'm grateful to be leaving the house, but the prospect of getting some fresh air to clear my head isn't the guarantee I'd hoped it would be. I'm cloudier than ever, overthinking every gesture and step, even as I shove the key into the ignition.

Santiago stiffens at the gentle roar of the engine. Even as I turtle down the driveway, his entire body is rigid. Flashes of Santos attacking the camera at the amusement park come back to me, and I worry Santiago might have a similar fit if he is pushed to his limit.

"The car is supposed to sound like that. It's one of

the many things you'll get used to in your new life. I'll drive slow, but it's probably going to feel scary for a bit." I glance toward him. "Fastening your seatbelt is a good idea."

I talk him through the mechanics of a seatbelt, grateful I can do that without actually buckling him in. I point out different buildings to distract him, explaining the basics of society.

This is a bank... That is a grocery store... There is a school...

The whole thing is boring to him, I'm sure, but he doesn't roll his eyes at me.

"Where are we going?" he finally asks when the silence sets in and builds to an uncomfortable level.

All my calm deserts me, and my nerves come out in a gust. "I'm La Ciguapa!"

That is not what he asked. He just wants to know where I'm taking him.

Yet once I start babbling, I can't stop myself. "I didn't mean to be La Ciguapa. Santos is my boyfriend, and I know you're probably thinking I scammed him, lured him in against his will, but you have to believe me that I didn't know! I fell for him long before I found out what I was. And somehow Santos knew what I was, and decided he was okay being with me regardless."

When Santiago blinks at me, I know I should stop talking.

Actually, I never should have started talking, but more floods out of me in a rampant confession that makes me sound unbalanced. "I have a second boyfriend! Cruz is also with me. Santos is cool with it, but it's weird. I know it's weird. It's probably not what you want for your brother, but I promise to be good to him. I'm learning, and sometimes I get it wrong, but I always want what's best for Santos. I'm sorry! I'm sorry."

I'm sweating now. Of course I am. Why wouldn't I make a fool of myself and also test the limits of my deodorant?

More comes out of me like bursts of vomit I can't hold back. "I stole his soul!"

The urge to bash my forehead on the steering wheel overcomes me, but I worry that would only frighten him more than I already am.

Santiago is hugging the door, his entire body itching to get away from me.

"I didn't know the rules of the Kalku, and I wanted a picture of the two of us. Santos doesn't speak up for himself, and I didn't take the time to listen. The camera took his picture, and I let it happen! I didn't know!"

Shut up! Shut up! Shut up!

"You blessed me two years ago, remember? Of

course you remember. You told me I'd only be as strong as I was gentle. I don't know if I let you down completely. I'm freaked out that you're disappointed, that you'll hate me and take away the limits of my strength. Please don't! I need that safeguard. I don't want to be a monster who strong-arms her way into getting what she wants."

Santiago holds up his hand to stop me, thank goodness. I'm fairly certain I could embarrass myself all day.

I pull over, my chest heaving at having confessed far too much.

That's it. That's the end of it. Santiago knows I'm a lunatic, and he's not going to give his blessing for me to be with his brother. I'll be the thing that drives a wedge between Santos and his brother.

I've ruined everything.

He mimes for me to lean forward so I can catch my breath. I consent, resting my forehead on the steering wheel while my breath decides if it wants to even out or not.

"I don't know how to help my own brother," Santiago admits.

It's not what I anticipated him saying.

I turn my chin toward Santiago, gaging his hesitance instead of the judgment I assumed I would receive. "Huh?"

"You all talk with your hands to him when he shuts down. I don't know how to do that. This Rafael person—I only met him the night he died. I worry Santos will never forgive me for costing him his friend." He bows his head. "I worry you'll never forgive me for not stopping the bus crash that killed your mother. I didn't cause it, but I knew it was going to happen and I didn't stop it. I was under orders to bring you in."

I blink at Santiago. For the first time, I realize he is just as nervous as I am.

"I don't blame you for my mother's death. You have to know that."

Santiago exhales slowly. "I do now."

My heart pounds at the mention of my mom. "You saved me that day. Not just in the crash, but Tavita told me you were supposed to bring me in, yet you let me go."

Santiago stares out the window, his eyes haunted. "I was punished most severely for that. I couldn't do it. I couldn't condemn you to the life I was stuck in. I don't regret that choice one bit. Only that I didn't have the courage to stop the crash before it happened."

Examining his sorrow, I can't help but lean toward him. "I think it's time we let that guilt be buried with Máximo, where it belongs." When he nods but tilts his head downward, I prod further. "What else is on your mind?"

"You all have such a system here. My twin brother has a whole life he's lived without me. I'm glad, of course. It's what I've hoped over and over—that Santos found his freedom and made good use of it. I just... I didn't expect he would have a life that didn't have a place for me."

I balk at him. "Oh, Santiago. No, no. There is a place here for you. It's supposed to feel weird right now. I didn't go through half of your upbringing, and I still had a hard time learning how I fit into Cáceres. Give yourself some grace. Some time. No one thinks you don't belong."

Santiago gives me a lighthearted "pfft" sound accompanied by a wry look that tells me he thinks I'm just being nice.

I sit up. "Cruz told me that Santos used to eat on the floor of the kitchen for the longest time. He felt the same way, I'd imagine—like the world he was in made very little sense, and he didn't know where or how he fit. But look at him now."

"You really think so?"

"I know so. Santos is incredible. If you're anything like him, all you need is time and a hand to hold while the world shifts around you. Trust me; you're more worried about your progress than anyone in the house ever will be."

His shoulders lower just enough to let me know he is listening to me, and I am (finally) saying something right. We stare at each other for a solid minute, letting the silence erase all the things that might break us more than we already are.

When the corner of Santiago's mouth lifts, it strikes me how much he looks like Santos. I mean, they're identical, but in the half-smile, I really see it.

"I already knew you were La Ciguapa. Who do you think told Tavita what she was?"

"You knew?" I balk at him, but then register with relief that he doesn't look upset at all, only amused at the source of my angst.

"Máximo had no one. He confessed a great many things to me, one of which was that his daughters were La Ciguapa by design. If he couldn't have sons, then he wanted daughters who could take down the most valiant of men."

My upper lip curls. "That's disgusting. As if Tavita or I would ever try to take down a man for sport. The only fighting we've ever done was for survival, not lust."

Santiago relaxes against his seat. "I guess Máximo didn't account for that. He assumed you'd both be like him." His tone takes on a teasing note that I don't know if I should like or not. "But I've seen how Commander Bruno is with Tavita. Malicious or not, she's taken him down. And while I don't know Cruz, I can surmise enough to guess that he's every bit the warrior people say he is. And Santos is no passive kitten. You've wrangled them both well enough for me to know Máximo was right. He was just counting on their attachment to you making them weak. That doesn't seem to be the case, though, does it."

I mull over his words, turning them this way and that so I can examine his statement from all angles. "I don't know what to say to that."

Santiago meets my eyes with a seriousness that stills my breath. "Say you'll be good to Santos. He has been through too much to be used and thrown away his whole life. Tell me you see him. Tell me he is a person to you, and not a slave."

A gasp flings out of me, my hand going over my heart. "I promise, Santiago. I love Santos. I would never throw him away."

Santiago nods without looking too bothered by the subject. "I know. Just putting it all out plainly, so we're both on the same page. Maybe we have more in common than I thought." Again, he treats me to that sneaky half-smile. "And you really thought you needed to apologize to me because you thought you stole Santos' soul with a picture?"

I swallow hard, afraid to answer. My fingers are hesitant when I start the car back up and pull onto the road.

"Do you have the photograph?"

I nod and motion to my wallet that's tucked in the cupholder between us. "It's in the longer section just there."

He slides out the photo, his lips parting as he takes in the image of me with his brother. I threw out the three others on the long black and white slip, but I kept the one where I'm smiling and Santos has his eyes closed, his forehead butted to my temple. I know that he was terrified, but I like to pretend there's a sweeter note to the photo.

Plus, given how poorly that event went, I'm guessing this will be the only picture I ever get of the two of us.

"Will I have this?" Santiago asks quietly while I drive us down a gravelly road.

"No. I won't take your picture, now that I know how scary it is for you and Santos. I shouldn't have done that in the first place. I didn't know any better. I would never do anything to purposefully hurt either of you."

Santiago sniggers, which I'll admit, I wasn't expecting. "I know that. I meant being with a woman like this.

Will I ever meet a woman I'm willing to give up my soul to be with?"

My mouth dries at his grand words. "Someday, yes. But hopefully she'll be the kind of woman who would never make you give up the important things about yourself." My voice takes on a gentler quality as I find my way back to myself. "Your whole life looks different right now, and it's going to take some getting used to. Take it one day at a time. When things get confusing, talk to us. Talk to Santos. Talk to me. We want you here. I've always wanted a brother."

Santiago beams at me. "Could that be what we are? Could you be my sister? I think I should like that very much."

My fingers quake as I reach over the console and touch his hand. "Absolutely. Right now, you and I are going to a diner to pick up milkshakes. That's a sweet sugary treat of ice cream blended with milk and syrup, and you drink it through a straw. Rafael had a goal of trying every flavor in the world, so every time we stopped anywhere, he ordered one of every kind of milkshake. He was never the type to hold back." I smile at the bittersweet memory. "Santos and Cruz might like some milkshakes. I doubt anyone is going to be hungry, but it might bring them a little piece of Rafael on a day they need it most."

"I like that idea. Tell me more. Tell me everything. Any little piece of my brother, I want to know it. Santos likes these milkshakes? He really drinks sugar?"

My spine relaxes against my seat as I drive us toward someplace familiar that I don't mind sharing with him. Maybe this will be our new language—the way we connect when everything feels scary and strange. We'll go for a drive and pick up milkshakes for the family together.

I like that.

For the next half hour, Santiago and I drink milkshakes and eat burgers, ordering a dozen milkshakes to go. He asks smart questions about Rafael, giving me a safe space where I can open up and unburden myself of the loss I feel at losing someone I love so dearly.

Santiago likes to hold my hand, I'm learning. He tangles his fingers through mine while I tell him our stories of fighting the Kalku on the road. We talk of the many ups and downs that led me to find my home in Cáceres.

When we drive back, Santiago doesn't let go of my hand. I don't blame him for needing the contact, someone to anchor him so he doesn't feel so very lost.

"Thank you," Santiago says quietly when I turn off the engine after I park in the garage. "That was the first time I forgot that I'm afraid."

I squeeze his fingers. "Hold onto me any time, okay?" I know the Kalku weren't ones for tender touches. He's been starved of sweetness for far too long.

Though there is a long way to go before the world evens out for either one of us, we hold tight to each other, knowing we won't sink if we lean on each other—the family we've created for ourselves.

14

FISH TACOS

CRUZ

I probably shouldn't wrap myself so tightly around Adelita under the sheets. I'm supposed to be sleeping, but I'm thinking my mind will be too preoccupied for rest tonight. It's been a week since Rafi's funeral, and I'm still not even close to calming myself down.

Adelita had to kiss each cadejo refugee they rescued from Máximo's island when our healers couldn't make heads or tails of the Chupacabras. One kiss from my girl, and each cadejo was cured. Their animals turned to something normal—a wide variety, in fact. Some wolves, one horse, and a panther. They had homes to return to, so our soldiers escorted them back to their lives.

But I made it clear that if any of the rescues had

nowhere to go, they would be offered lodging in Cáceres. There was much murmuring about that, but in the end, my big stand was a moot point, because every rescue wanted to get back to their normal lives as quickly as possible.

It's been a long week.

I cannot imagine Adelita is comfortable like this, with me practically on top of her, my legs and arms twined around her in what can only be described as a restraint. Without her as close as humanly possible, I worry I'll drift into the abyss in my mind I'm too scared to touch.

Rafi is dead.

Even the thought makes me wince.

Adelita pats my arm awkwardly. "You want to talk about it, sweetheart?"

No. No and never. I don't want to talk about Rafi's death that I wasn't even there for. I don't want to talk about his empty bedroom. I don't want to talk about any of it.

But that's not really an option when you're dating a therapist.

Santos is in Santiago's room at the moment, otherwise he would be a fantastic distraction for her. Without him nearby, my grief is palpable, and not as easy to hide.

I loosen my hold on her just enough for her body to

relax, but I know if I let go completely, I'll drift into my dark oblivion.

"Just wrapping my mind around it, I guess. Rafi's gone. He's my brother, and he's dead. I can't..." I orbit my hand around my head. "I'm still processing, I guess. It's all too big to wrap my mind around."

"That makes sense." She rubs a spot between my eyebrows. I didn't even realize I needed her touch in that exact spot. She's good like that—sensing the problem and slowly unwinding it for me.

She doesn't smell like herself tonight. I need her to smell like roses, as she always does.

My next confession slips out before I can clamp my mouth shut. "I'm worried I'm going crazy."

She stops moving altogether. "Well, that's a new one. Explain."

"It's like Rafi's still here, moving my stuff around just to piss me off. My knife was in my boot the wrong way. I always have the blade toward my toe, but it was facing my heel yesterday. That's not a mistake I make."

Her frown affects me more than I'd like to admit. "You're so hard on yourself."

"Not just my knife. My glass of water was drained, but I know I had some left." I roll over onto my back, but I don't like being parted from her, so I drape her arm across my stomach. "More likely the reason my things are moved to places I don't remember putting them is because I'm losing my mind."

She doesn't argue with me; she's too smart for that. Instead she rubs my stomach in slow circles. "That sounds stressful."

"It is. I should be relaxing, but I can't calm down. I'm used to always being on the road. This grieving thing doesn't suit me."

Dead. Rafi's dead.

I shiver as the gong of reality hits me over the head, as it so often does when I'm least expecting it. I still feel a foreign presence watching me, though it doesn't always bring me comfort. Not much does these days, except being wound tightly around Adelita.

Santos is still with Santiago. He usually comes to bed with us around midnight, when he's certain Santiago is asleep and doesn't need anything.

I cannot imagine his stress level right now.

"Roll over," Adelita prods, giving me a light shove.

I comply, though I can't imagine how being further away from her is going to help. I hate the meager space between us the second the air hits my skin.

I don't expect her to straddle my butt. When her hands roam over my back, massaging the muscle that's been too tight for much fluid movement, all tension leaves me in a gust. I groan like a dying whale into my pillow, foregoing decorum because she's just that good.

"Your back is like a sack of rocks, babe. I don't know how anyone could be expected to sleep like this. I'll rub them out for you."

Whatever she says, I'll do. Her touch is the only medicine I need. I love everything about this, especially the care she takes with me. I'm never cautious with what my body goes through, but Addy cares. I love that. She works her magic on me, kneading my muscles until I'm practically purring for her.

I'm grateful Santos isn't seeing me like this: lips parted, drool beginning to form, and humping the mattress whenever Addy hits a sweet spot.

My eyelids are nearly shut when the door opens and Santos slips in. He's back to not speaking aloud, so I use every effort to keep my eyes open in case he needs to sign something.

"Santiago's not doing well with his mattress. He's used to sleeping in the dirt. Keeps thinking he's going to fall off the bed. Says there's a ghost about. I'm going to sleep with him so he calms down."

I relay the message to Addy, though she's getting pretty good at interpreting.

I should let Santos go, but honestly, it's not fair that I get a massage and he has to go sleep with a dude. "Bring

Santiago in here. The bed's plenty big enough for a fourth."

Adelita nods. "Of course, Santos. If he's afraid, bring him in here. The two of you shouldn't be separated when you're both going through a crisis."

I love when she talks like that—all smart and authoritative.

Santos pauses, taking in the tenor of the room to make sure we're serious. Then he kneels next to us on the mattress and kisses Adelita softly to express his gratitude. They're so sweet together, and here I am, ready to moan like a cow giving birth when she touches me next.

When Santos comes back with Santiago, Adelita has massaged me into total submission. If she wanted me to do just about anything, I would attempt it for her. She climbs off of me for decorum's sake, offering Santiago a welcoming smile as she crosses her legs atop the mattress. She looks like a teenager readying for a slumber party.

Santiago is a welcome addition. Just when we lost Rafi, a fourth shows up to divert my creeping depression. Santiago is the constant project, just like Santos was when he first arrived. Though I've only known the man a week, I can already tell he's a good fit for us. Santiago is more inquisitive than his twin, which tells me he cares enough about his new life to attempt having one for himself.

The only thing I'm still getting used to is how often he and Addy hold hands. I get it, and it's a good thing, but it sticks in my brain when it probably shouldn't. He holds onto Tavita, too. He's looking for a safe port in the storm, which I can't begrudge the guy.

Santiago casts us a sheepish look. "You sure this is okay?"

Adelita moves her pillow toward mine to make room for him. Though really, she and Santos always end up on the same pillow by the time the sun rises. "Of course. You're in a new place, Santiago. It'll take some time getting used to everything. Be patient with yourself. Good for you for asking for what you need."

Santiago sets his pillow on the furthest edge. "Santos and I used to sleep side-by-side in the caves. I had the hardest time on the island without him. Not to mention that sleeping in the back of a cave is different than on a wide-open island where there's a breeze coming straight at you. And the moon is too bright." He waves off his words. "I'll get used to a mattress."

Santos claps his brother's shoulder twice and signs a quick reply.

"Santos says that you don't need to rush yourself. You can sleep with us as long as you like. Whatever he has is yours." I hate interpreting for a family member. Santos is grieving, of course, so I don't push him, but it's only going to make Santiago more on edge, not hearing his brother's voice.

Santiago's hurt over not understanding his twin's secret language splashes across his features, but he covers it over with a meek, "Thanks."

Santiago casts Adelita furtive glances. I can't tell if he's nervous to be around her, or if he's nervous for her, like he thinks she's in danger or something. He's been hovering for days. I'm not sure if it's creepy or if he's just found his safe person, like Santos did when he latched onto me and Rafi when he first arrived.

I roll over and invite Adelita to rest in my arms while we both wind down for the night. Though she's already done her part to calm me down, I'm not sure I'll ever stop craving more. She sedates my unrest better than a shot of mezcal.

Santiago and Santos settle in while I kiss my girlfriend, trying not to be too sloppy about it and make a scene. I love the way she tastes, and the way her lips lose their rhythm when she's sleepy.

She turns to kiss Santos goodnight, and twists around so she can burrow her butt into Santos' lap, welcoming me to curl into her front.

Ah, bliss.

Santiago sits up on his elbow, eyeing Adelita with that same worry he's had for days. "Can I check something?"

Adelita sits up. "Of course. What do you need?"

"Can you just..." He reaches over Santos and slides his hand through Addy's hair, pulling it back over her shoulder so he can peer at the scope of her throat.

What the fates is he doing?

He's so close to her now, leaning over Santos like he's been granted full access to her body.

I sit up, determined to not be an overprotective controlling bully to my girlfriend, but letting everyone in the room know that if she merely whimpers, I'll intervene in ways no one is going to like.

I want to get along with Santiago. I want my brother's brother to be my family, too.

Santiago sniffs the air near Adelita's neck curiously, like he's trying to decipher notes in a glass of wine.

"Pishtaco," he whispers, as if that's supposed to mean anything to us.

Santos stiffens. "No. No, that's not possible. She's been with us this entire time."

My eyebrows bunch. It occurs to me there are worse things than a man sniffing around my girlfriend, and Santiago might be more aware of them than I am. "What are you talking about? What's wrong?"

Addy's nose scrunches cutely. "You're hungry? You want fish tacos? I can go pick some up for you."

Santiago shakes his head. "You smell like Pishtaco."

Her shoulders slump. "I smell like fish tacos? Great. I'm taking a shower."

Santiago catches her arm before she leans forward to exit. "You smell like death. Pishtaco has been near you."

She pinches the bridge of her nose. "I didn't think anything could be worse than stinking like fish tacos, but smelling like death just might beat that. I'll be back in a few."

Santos' arms go around her to still her parting, his nose burying deep in her hair, then her neck and shoulder.

Curious, I take the other side, running my nose along her skin. Sure enough, there's a faint hint of... something that doesn't smell like my Addy. Guess I was too wrapped up in my grief to take issue with it before. "What is that?"

Her eyes roll back as her head tilts toward the headboard. "Mm. Guys, I really don't think we should give Santiago a show."

I run my hand along her thigh, unable to help myself.

Santos and I pull away. While I'm uncertain of what

I'm smelling, Santos appears convinced of something grave.

Great. Just what we need.

Santos' fingers flick with rapid angst, leaving me to interpret for the room. While Addy understands a fair bit of sign language now, he's speaking so fast, even I am having a hard time keeping up.

"Pishtaco is a Kalku myth that even they don't believe is true. It's a twist of theoretical magic. It's a man undead who finds a way to rise up, but he remains unseen. He craves the fat of his offspring, because he's mostly comprised of invisible skin and bones when he first arises. He'll drain your fat so he can take form. He's pale, his skin forever white." He pauses for our shudder. "After he takes form by draining the fat of his offspring, he can survive by feeding off the fat of anyone."

I don't think this story can get any worse until Santiago motions to Addy. "Pishtaco stinks like death. He has been near my sister."

My hand touches on the middle of Addy's back. I can feel her heartrate picking up, thumping wildly.

Santos closes his eyes, signing, "*Máximo. Tio Bruno was supposed to destroy the emeralds that held the Luz Mala. Did anyone check on that?*"

Adelita's voice comes out frightened as she tugs the

comforter up to cover her chest. "You told me Tavita ripped Máximo's heart out. You said he was dead."

"He was," Santiago supplies. Then his eyes close. "The Luz Mala went out, but if the emeralds weren't destroyed in time, Máximo's specter might have taken shape." Santiago's chin lowers. "I've been watching you like a hawk, Adelita. I was worried something like this might happen. Máximo used to talk about his backup plan, should any of us try to kill him. I didn't realize this would be his route. It takes a fair bit of darkness in a man's soul to be able to rise undead like that." He lets out a "pfft" sound. "Then again, you have to murder a hundred souls to create a Luz Mala, so using Pishtaco as a backup plan isn't too far off the map for his character."

"Tavita," Adelita breathes. "We have to get Tavita somewhere safe. Right now. Tonight. If I'm in danger, so is she. And we have to destroy those emeralds."

I stand, pulling on my jeans. I guess we're not sleeping tonight. "How do we kill a Pishtaco? Tavita already ripped out Máximo's heart, so I'm guessing the normal ways to kill a man aren't going to be all that effective if we're dealing with something that's already dead. Or undead, as the case may be."

Santos finally speaks. It's been days, but this is the thing that brings him back to us. "To kill Pishtaco, you have to set his bones on fire."

At this, my sweet Addy bursts into tears. Frankly, I'm surprised it's taken this long. She held herself back during the funeral, being there for us, bringing milkshakes and entertaining Santiago so Santos and I could grieve. But this—her dad partially coming back to life and needing to suck the fat from her body? It's too much for anyone to stomach.

Santos and I melt into her sides. We can't help it. Any sort of planning is put on hold at first sight of my woman's tears.

Santiago stands from the bed, his face serious as he roams about the room, his arms outstretched to try his hand at locating someone invisible.

Santos kisses her shoulder, and I know that, aside from wanting to comfort her, he's also attempting to erase the scent of the Pishtaco from her and replace it with his own.

I can't believe how hard-hearted I was before Adelita, and how much I've grown. I dab at her tears with the pad of my thumb, holding her close while she trembles like a fluttering leaf. Life is once again being cruel to her. My chest swells because she comes to us when she needs a place to hide away from the cruelty.

This is the kind of protection I never knew I could give. I'm better with knives, with fists. But when the thing that's needed is tenderness, I'm usually not the person for the job.

Except now I am. I've grown so much that I know how to handle this upset, even though it's unbalanced my own footing just as much.

"Santiago, can you pack us a few changes of clothes? We need to get her away from the house, away from the kids. The bunker has concrete cells we can hole up in for a while until we figure out a plan." The longer I hold Addy in my arms, the easier the plan comes to me. "Don't go to your room to pack clothes. We can't chance anyone separating us from her. You're around Santos' size, so pack yourself some of his clothes for yourself. My knives are atop the dresser. Those, too. I know you're not used to shoes yet, but sandals aren't going to do you any good in a brawl, especially one that might involve fire. Santos has a spare pair of boots in the closet. Try them on. If they don't fit, you can try some of mine."

Adelita sobs in my arms as Santos lets go to help his brother pack us up. She doesn't hold back for our comfort, like she usually does.

"My dad is only coming for me so he can drain my fat!" she wails, her tears wetting my naked chest.

My palm rubs up and down her arm. She's always the beacon of calm when one of us falls apart. Finally, it's my turn to anchor her. "No, Addy. Your father's name is José, not Máximo. Your dad loves you and celebrates you. Máximo is nothing to you. He is not your family. We are."

Still she sobs, overcome by everything that has proved to be too much.

Santos and Santiago move seamlessly about the room like a well-rehearsed dance. They're both agile, graceful and light on their feet, communicating almost psychically while they stuff necessities into backpacks.

Addy doesn't want to be parted from me for the smallest of seconds, so I don't bother trying to get her dressed for the trip outside. Instead, I wrap the comforter around her and hoist her up in my arms. I love the weight of her, the substantial feel of her curves. If one ounce went missing, I would mourn the loss.

She lets me take care of her, which is a shocker I don't pause to examine. I take the gift and run with it, leading the way out of the house and into the night—my treasure in my arms and my brothers by my side.

15

FAT, FAMILY AND FIRE
ADELITA

I can't get ahold of myself. My center is so far from me that I can barely keep my sobs quiet as Cruz carries me, wrapped in our comforter, toward the barracks.

"There's nothing to worry about if I'm here," he reminds me, but I've passed the point of reason.

My undead father wants to hunt me down so he can suck the fat from my body, ensuring that he can walk the earth for a second time. His skin will be white, not a medium umber, like mine. The very thought makes me shudder.

There's no calming down from this. I can feel eyes on me, though I know I've simply lost my mind. An invisible pale man-ghost made of only skin and bones with no fat to him is hunting me down. He's gotten close already, marking me with his scent.

Terror streaks through me every time I picture the fat being sucked out of my body. That my father is only tracking me down to use me and possibly kill me in the process?

I miss my mother horribly. There is no part of me that can process all of this. I need her to hold me and snuggle me on the couch while we do our nails. I need her to make churros and horchata and tell me everything is going to be alright. She could figure a way through anything—poverty, sickness, snobbery. She was unstoppable.

And right now, I am utterly lost.

Cruz hands me to Santos when we reach the barracks, unlocking a cell door so we can bolt ourselves inside.

I hate this place. The concrete walls and ceiling create a chill that never goes away. No wonder Tio Bruno was always so cross when he lived here; he was freezing. There is no beauty anywhere—only gray nothingness.

Santos' mind is on keeping us safe as he sizes up the cell. It's far too small for four people to share without getting in each other's way, but being that I refuse to leave the arms of either Santos or Cruz, that hardly matters.

I shiver in Santos' lap as he sits on the cot that's butted up against the wall. He is the wealth of calm now, so I drink from the slow way he rubs his palm up and down my spine. I bury my nose in his neck, so I can inhale his scent while I cry.

Santos doesn't speak when Cruz locks the three of us in here and then steps out of the room so he can call Tio Bruno and Tavita to alert them of the danger.

A low sound distracts me from my terror. A beautiful melody that must be from the heavens drifts through the cell, cutting my sobs short.

"IN THE DARK *of the woods, I can hear your cry.*
In the valley so deep, I can count your sighs.
No matter where you go, or hide the way you do,
I will never stop my search. I will always come for you."

AGAIN, the song repeats from Santiago's lips, but this time, Santos sings the song too. On the third repeat, they harmonize, and I'm fairly certain I've never heard any sound more hauntingly beautiful than this.

When they finish, Santiago's whisper is choked. "I have missed you every day since we were parted, Santos. My only hope that got me through was knowing you'd been given a better life. I never dreamed you would have all this—a new family and a woman in your arms who trusts you like this."

Santos' voice is gravelly with emotion. "This life is yours now, too. I thought you were dead. I'm not sure I'll ever forgive myself for that. I shouldn't have believed my eyes."

Santiago tugs at the collar of his shirt, pulling it to the side to display a long, jagged scar. "You thought this little scratch could kill me?"

The two share a smile.

"I can f-fix that," I offer through hiccupped tears.

Santos tangles his fingers in my hair. "Later," he instructs. "When Santiago has time to deal with the pain of it, then that would be much appreciated. But if Máximo is hunting you, we need Santiago on his game."

Santiago quirks his brow. "You can heal a scar? What for? It's already healed."

Santiago motions to his cheek. "Who do you think smoothed out the scarring I used to have on my face?"

Santiago frowns and then studies me curiously. "Are you a surgeon?"

I shake my head but still hold tight to Santos. "No.

My kisses heal wounds, but I guess it's super painful. Takes a few hours of agony to iron out something deep."

Santos combs his fingers through my hair. "How do you think the shifters from the island were really cured? It was Adelita, going to them and kissing them, healing their animals so the men could have control over their beasts."

Santiago gasps. "You did that? I thought it was some village medicine or something."

I burrow into Santos. "I can heal your scar when the business with Máximo is figured out. It's painful, but it works."

"Like it never happened?" There is agonized hope in Santiago's eyes.

"A clean slate," I confirm. I hold Santiago's gaze for a few beats before he stands, placing his body between us and the door.

When Cruz comes back in, I can tell he is tired, judging by his slower movements. "Want me to bring in a chair, Santiago?"

"I'm good. I've been by her side all week to make sure Pishtaco didn't come for her. I'm not about to take a break now."

Cruz's shoulders lower. "That's why you've been around her all the time?"

Santiago nods once, as if wondering what other

reason there could be. "Of course. She is precious to Santos, so I guard her with my life. I don't know how Máximo got close to her. I've been so careful to stay close everywhere she goes. I won't let it happen again."

Cruz looks so relieved. I wonder just how often he is completely stressed out by all he internalizes. Without warning, he wraps Santiago in a hug I can tell the man isn't used to receiving.

"Thank you," Cruz says while he grips Santiago tight. "I thought... It doesn't matter what I thought. I'm glad you're here. I'm grateful for the help."

Santiago is stunned at first, frozen on the spot, but finally his arms find their way around Cruz. "Anything you need, please tell me. I'm quite useful. I will protect my sister to the death. If you are my brother's brother, then you are my family, too. Sit down, Cruz. Rest. I will take the first watch."

Cruz kisses Santiago's cheek before releasing him from the hug.

I love witnessing such unfettered affection.

Cruz moves to the floor, since there isn't room on the cot. I don't like the sight of him there, but Santos keeps me firmly on his lap, as if he knows I'm about to offer Cruz the bed and take the spot on the floor.

When a knock sounds at the door, Cruz gets up to answer it. "Tio Bruno. You made it. Good. Hey, Tavita."

Santiago hugs Tavita while Tio Bruno and Cruz converse. I can tell Santiago is sniffing around Tavita's neck to search for traces of the undead.

Gross. This whole thing is disgusting.

"You alright, Sis?" I ask her.

Tavita shivers. "Am I okay? Not really. I mean, I was about to go to sleep and then found out my dead dad wasn't so dead. I'm upright. That's about as good as it gets right now, people."

I know the feeling.

She shakes her head at herself. "I'm so sorry we didn't destroy those emeralds. In the mess of coming home and the funeral and everything, it slipped our minds. We destroyed them just now before we came, though, so once Pishtaco is dead, he's not coming back."

Tio Bruno glances around the cell. "This won't do. If we're together in this, we need to actually be able to move around. We have to be able to start a fire without lighting ourselves up in the process." He jerks his head toward the hallway. "My place in the bunker is bigger and just as secure."

When everyone stands to leave, and Santos is certain I can amble around on my own, I finally speak up. "No. That's not a good idea."

Tio Bruno pauses, looking me over and no doubt picking up on the bedraggled details of my appearance:

puffy eyes, tear-stained face, and wrapped in a bulky comforter. "You've got a better idea for a safe place, half-pint?"

"A safe place isn't a better idea. I want this over with. I want to smoke Máximo out. I'm not going into hiding like this. If Máximo wants to suck the fat from my body so he can more fully come back to life, then let's get on with it. Give me a stick of butter and let me go stand in the middle of the village. You all can light him on fire when he comes for me."

Tavita glares at me, which I'll admit, I didn't expect. "No. No and never. You're not going to be live bait, Addy."

Tio Bruno tilts his head to the side, considering my path. "I mean, it's not a terrible idea."

Tavita's eyes bug. "Are you kidding me with this? It's suicide!"

"I'm being hunted either way," I counter. "At least this way, you all can be ready for him. You can be hiding in the periphery and ambush him when he strikes. That way we control the fight."

Tavita's lips press together in clear displeasure. "Not a chance. You just lost someone, Addy. You're not thinking clearly. I'll go. I'll be the bait."

At this, I raise myself up, finally able to stand for myself. "Santiago, has Máximo come near Tavita yet?"

Santiago shakes his head. "I can't smell him on her. Tavita ended his life. I'm guessing he's more than a little wary of her."

That seals it. "Then I'll go. Get whatever supplies you need. I'm going to the village square because there aren't trees nearby or any homes for the fire to catch on." The fear that so consumed me minutes ago is still there, but it's quieter now. "Let's end this once and for all."

16

BAIT
ADELITA

I talked a good game in there, acting all calm when I voiced my idea to the others, but now that I'm standing in the middle of the village square, I'm certain my trembling is noticeable.

Usually I can rely on my unnatural strength to get me out of brawls, but this is different. My father is a skeleton with skin, and the only reason he wants to be near me is because he wants to suck the fat from my body so he can come more fully back to life.

Not quite the picturesque family moment I'd hoped for when I was a little girl.

I've never seen Máximo. I don't know what my own father looks like. Do I have his nose? The determination in my eyes I thought came from my mother, but since

Máximo is bent on haunting me after death, perhaps that's his marker on my genetics.

My jeans and black t-shirt are not enough to fend off the shiver that rips through me when the night air reminds me I should have donned a sweater. The middle of the night is no time to be reading a book by flashlight on a bench, but that's exactly what I'm doing, lighting the path that leads directly to me.

My heart hammers so loudly, I'm certain the pounding rhythm will give everything away. Santos is in the bushes to my left. Cruz is hiding to my right. Santiago is guarding Tavita, while Tio Bruno watches both Tavita and me from afar.

I have no idea what my book is about. Tio Bruno handed it to me from his bunker. It's got a bunch of war strategies laid out, but I couldn't want to understand anything less than I do this nonsense. I don't want a life of war. I want hot chocolate and sleeping in the same bed for a solid month.

I've got some lofty goals, I know.

I'm exhausted, and the ruse of reading isn't convincing anyone. I set the book down at the end of the bench and lay my head on it, using the thing as a pillow. I can practically hear Tio Bruno grumbling at the sight.

My body curls up as much as I am able. Though I'm

still shivering, I close my eyes and will calmness into my breathing. In and out, my breath finds a way to steady.

It's been a long road. I wonder if things will start to get easier after this.

With Rafael's funeral, there's been no talk of going after the Kalku, frantic as they must be without their leader. That will be the thing we throw ourselves into next. And after that, who knows? Something will arise that pulls us into action. For now, I try to enjoy the inaction that lulls my limbs to motionlessness. It flees all too quickly for my comfort.

I try not to stiffen when, after at least an hour, the cracking of a twig from behind stiffens my spine. Even though I'm not facing him, I know it's my father. I've never known what his feet sound like when he comes home from work, what his aftershave smells like, but this snap of a twig is instinctual and clear as it echoes through my mind.

My eyes are shut, feigning sleep even as what feels like a breeze shifts my hair over my shoulder to reveal my neck.

What is taking them so long? Fire already! Attack him!

I lay perfectly still, making sure to give them a clear shot. It's not until something hard presses on the juncture between my neck and shoulder that I open my eyes.

My chin turns, bringing the full breadth of my skeletal father into view. He's gaunt, his skin as white as snow. I've never seen anything like it. Everyone in the world is varying shakes of brown, but this white face comes at me, sucking a necessary resource I cannot survive without. He knows this, yet he doesn't care. My father has always been selfish, but this is a new level of sadistic.

His mouth is bony as he sucks. The more he drinks, the less translucent he becomes.

My scream is frozen on my lips as a sensation I've never before endured floods my system, accompanied by fresh terror. It's like all laughter, light and life are being drained from me, weighting my limbs so that all I can do is grieve and panic.

The first long pull he takes is finished with a slurp that sickens me down to my soul.

I can't move, can hardly breathe. Everything is too heavy now. I'm not sure I could scream for help, much less run away.

I don't know what he looks like. Not really. This can't be him. He's barely a person, more a like a skeleton with bleached skin stretched too thin to be useful.

Máximo goes in for a second hit, but he never makes contact. My father's scream grates my ears, slicing the air as he jerks forward, his bony body bending over the back of the bench onto me.

The guys and Tavita rush him, hitting him with arrows, knives, and finally, a torch.

Santos comes at Máximo with a flame, his eyes dancing with malice because part of him will always be savage. Máximo made it so.

I relish that part of the man I love, holding it tight in my heart even as my clothes catch fire when Máximo's blaze leaps onto my body.

I can't move. Something about Máximo's assault took the fight from my limbs.

I feel the bite of the burns as the scene blurs out of focus. The bony body is hoisted off of me, but it's too late. The bite has done something foul. I can feel it leaking through my bloodstream, taking me away from the family I love.

My eyes close, and finally, I am taken away even from myself.

I didn't expect to go out like this.

17

UNDERGROUND HEALERS
CRUZ

I didn't know what to do. There's no medicinal help in the village for whatever it was Máximo did to his own daughter. I panicked, and I'm not ashamed to admit it. Scooping Adelita in my arms and running to the car seemed like the right move at the time.

Too many hours into the trek, I'm not sure if there is any path that will make things better for her.

I grabbed Eva from her bedroom, waking her with no explanation other than, "I need help."

She asked no questions but got dressed and shoved herself into the car with Santos and Santiago, who seem to come as a pair now. After we were on the road, then the questions came. The story of Máximo becoming a

Pishtaco unfolded, ending with a shriek of horror when Eva peeled back the blanket covering Adelita.

I've been sick to my stomach ever since.

"He can help us," I say again, though it's brought me no more reassurance than it did the first several times I said the phrase aloud. "Their medicine is better than ours."

Though I'm not sure anyone's ever seen anything like this.

Eva keeps her voice as steady as possible. She's a good sister, and she knows I'm on the edge of sanity as it is. "Tio Bruno and Tavita stayed behind to make sure Máximo's bones are burned?"

"Yes. It's taken care of."

Santos has his healer's bag, but even he is at a loss. He can usually treat any malady with a stoic look about him, but I've caught sight of his tears each time I've peeked in the rearview mirror.

Santiago and Santos speak in hushed tones, checking on her bandaged burns every so often. When Tavita calls me again to see if her sister has awoken, I have no good news for her.

Eva's call to Salvador was quick and to the point. He'll be ready for us when we get there.

I barely slow before slamming on the brakes once we get there. We were marked as criminals when we came to Anzaldúa before, but this time I have no patience for the ruse.

Luckily, Salvador seems to have prepped his people for our entrance, so no one looks antsy to arrest us. On the contrary, they have a stretcher ready and several people with healer bags who greet us with serious faces, ready to offer their assistance.

"Don Salvador," I greet him. After I killed his brutal ruler of a father, the tribe fell into his care. "Thank you for helping us."

Santos and Santiago start rattling off medical stats to the team, saying words like "unresponsive," "badly burned," and "system in shock."

They move her gurney into a building that looks like it sells marbles, but I know that's just a front. All the businesses along this long underground stretch of road are decoys, meant to keep their living quarters underneath a secret from possible invaders.

Salvador grips my shoulder as the twins follow the gurney into the building. "They'll do everything they can to save her. We've never come across a Pishtaco before, so their treatment is based half in reality and half in myth."

The moment the Marble Emporium door shuts, my knees give way. I don't realize I'm collapsing until my knees hit the ground.

"Whoa! Cruz, it's okay. Salvador is going to help us now." Eva's voice does nothing to calm me, though I know she's trying her best. "Salvador, is there a place he can lay down? He's been going all night. It's been a dreadful week for our family."

Salvador's voice is gravelly. "Of course. This way. I'm guessing you don't want to be too far from the Marble Emporium?"

"I should be in there," I argue, my hands pressed to the dirt as I steady myself on all fours.

Eva rubs my back. "You should lie down. Let the healers do their thing. Santos is with her, Cruz. He'll watch over her."

Salvador and my sister help me to my feet and lead me to the building two down from where Adelita rests. The sign over the entrance brags that it sells the "Best Horchata in Town", but I know that's a front, too.

Salvador nods at the clerk. "My guests need some water, Pedro. He's going to lie down on your sofa in the back, alright?"

Pedro hurriedly moves to help us. I feel like such a tool, growing faint because... because...

Because I lost my brother last week, and then watched my girlfriend nearly die from an attack administered by her undead father, and then drove all night to get her help.

Come to think of it, I'm surprised I haven't actually passed out yet.

Salvador and Eva sit me down on the sofa while Pedro presses a glass of water into my palm. "Let me know if you need something stronger. Don Salvador told us of your victory over Máximo. Whatever you want, it's yours. Our tribe owes you a great debt."

I nod to Pedro. "Thanks, man. Just the water is fine for now."

Eva takes charge. "Actually, my brother hasn't eaten much in days. Would you mind getting him and Santos something to eat? Santos is helping with the healers, but at least give him the option of food."

I'm grateful Eva is here, thinking of things I'm forgetting to worry about.

Salvador sits in a chair opposite the sofa. "I'm forever grateful to you, Cruz. Anything we can do to help your Ciguapa, we will do."

"I'm screwing this all up," I blurt out the moment Pedro is gone from the room, leaving just the three of us together in the quaint back office. "I don't know what I'm doing anymore!"

Eva sits beside me, her hand on my back. "You did the right thing, bringing Adelita here. You cannot control the fates, or Máximo's hold on magic."

"I let her offer herself up as bait. I knew it was a bad

idea, but I let it happen. Now she's fighting for her life in there, and I can't do a thing to save her! I'm in no position to take care of a tribe. I can't even protect my own girlfriend!"

Eva shushes me, holding me from the side as she begins to rock me back and forth. "This is not the week to be cruel to yourself. Máximo has escaped everyone's reach for a century. You are the one who took him down. All we can hope now is that Rafi was his last casualty."

At mention of our dead brother, a sob escapes me, polluting the air before I can stuff it back inside.

"Cruz, this is not your fault. You can only be responsible for saving so many people."

"Adelita is my person! She is the one I should have saved. Rafi was my person. I should have been able to save him. I never should've let him go over to the island without me."

My sister holds me while I break down. And as much as I wish Salvador would go away, he stays with us, bringing in food and a blanket to make sure I want for nothing.

Adelita is fading, and I can't save her.

Salvador squats in front of me, getting in my eyeline. "There is nothing we will not do to help you, Cruz. You've delivered the world from Máximo's grip, and you helped me when I was too scared to do the right thing for Anzaldúa."

I know Salvador is referring to when I murdered his incapacitated father, but I'm glad he veils his speech. We don't need that getting out.

Despite my insistence that I don't want to sleep, after a few bites of a sandwich, Eva lays me down on the sofa and spreads a blanket over me. Then she and Salvador sit on the other side of the room, whispering to each other things like, "I cannot be parted from you any longer," and "Uniting our tribes is the only way we can be together."

I can't deal with that headache right now. I'm not sure I actually fall asleep, but I rest my eyes and my body until Santos comes in, rousing me from the sofa.

I cannot read his face. There's no joy, but there's also no devastation.

"Is she okay? Is she alive?" I ask, certain that parts of me are coming unhinged.

Santos doesn't answer, but instead wraps his arms around me, holding me tight while he inhales a nervous breath.

"Tell me what's happened!" I wail, unable to stand the suspense any longer.

"She's fragile, but she'll live. They're brilliant, Cruz. I've never seen healers like this. I'm learning so much.

You did the right thing, bringing her to Anzaldúa. I was so scared. I froze and didn't know what to do when I saw her like that. You did. You always do." Santos breaks down in my arms, finally crying out his anxiety on my shoulder.

I grip the back of his head, holding him tight because I know his pain well.

"I was so scared!" he says again, then another time, stuck in a loop now that he has found a safe place to unload.

Eva tends to Santos much in the same way she did me. She waves me off, so I can go check on Addy and see the miracle for myself.

I need to see her face. I have to know the sun still rises in her eyes whenever she sees me.

I have to know our life didn't break her.

18

THE FUTURE OF CÁCERES
SANTOS

I can't remember the last time I slept a full night through. Between Rafael's passing, Santiago coming home, and Adelita being bedridden, I'm not sure I'll ever sleep soundly again. I'm still dripping from my shower, the underground chill settling deep in my bones no matter how hot I cranked the nozzle. I fish through my pack for cleanish clothes with a towel around my waist when Cruz enters the bedroom Salvador gave us to share in his subterranean home.

"Adelita sat up on her own this morning," Cruz informs me as he stretches his arms over his head. "The healer said that once she can walk around, we can take her home. Shouldn't be too many more days now."

"That's good. I don't know how Anzaldúa does it, living underground like this. I haven't seen the sun in a week, and it's starting to grate on me." I usually don't make a habit of complaining, but the fluorescent lights do nothing for my mood. I need actual sunlight. "Is Eva still out with Don Salvador?"

Cruz nods once, his movement jerky. I don't think he's all that fond of Salvador, but then again, Cruz isn't fond of many people. He prefers the few friends he knows he can count on. Anyone else has a long road of proving themselves if they want a shot at being in his inner circle of trust. Though, being that Cruz brought Adelita here for healing, he must trust Salvador more than most. Perhaps more than he realizes.

The knock on our door hurries my movements as I slide my underwear and jeans on.

Cruz answers the door while I finish getting dressed. "Lady Eva requests your presence in Adelita's room. Both of you."

Cruz nods, dismissing the messenger. "You coming?"

"Of course."

Santiago is only half an hour into his shift with Adelita, watching over her to make sure she has all she needs, but I don't need a break. The healer came up with the schedule because he said the way Cruz and I were attached to her wasn't healthy.

Ridiculous.

I hate that we were sent away, and relish a smug upward tilt of my nose when we are summoned back.

Cruz and I move through the hallways. They have been lit with lanterns that hang along the walls. We're getting better at navigating the unmarked corridors, but I'm glad Cruz is with me, just in case I get lost again.

We make it to Adelita's sick room after having made only two wrong turns. Worry churns my stomach, wondering if the reason we were summoned is because her condition has somehow worsened.

Relief floods me when my eyes connect with hers. Her cheeks, though thinned out, have color in them. Máximo sucked out a fair bit of fat, leaving her far thinner than anyone would like. But with the Anzaldúa healers, she seems to be on the right path to recovery.

Still, I kiss the top of her head, testing her temperature. I fluff her pillow because, honestly, how has no one done that?

Cruz is right behind me, propping her feet up on a spare pillow and making sure her toes don't get chilly.

"Guys, I'm okay."

I don't disrespect her by arguing, but it's clear she's not. Adelita is skin and bones now, having lost too much fat far too fast. Her face is gaunt and every movement looks like it would cause her pain.

I should never have left to shower.

"Everything alright?" Cruz asks his sister, who's sitting on the bed beside Adelita on her other side, with Salvador standing nearby.

Santiago offers his seat next to her bed to me, but I recognize the gesture as being that of a slave, and not of a man who deserves a seat.

"No, no, Santiago. You sit. We'll stand."

Santiago doesn't like the idea, but he obeys.

Eva smiles at us with happiness dancing in her usually haughty gaze. I've always admired her confidence, yet this slice of vulnerability adds a fresh layer to the sister who has always accepted the mess that I am. "Everything's great, actually. Salvador and I..." She looks over her shoulder at Salvador, who hasn't left her side since we got here.

Cruz stiffens but doesn't say a word. It's clear she doesn't know how to voice the reason she called us down here, fiddling with Adelita's sleeve as she is. The more she fusses over Adelita, the more I realize how very nervous Eva is.

"What's wrong?" I ask Eva. "Whatever it is, I will fix it."

Eva's hand moves to her heart as she smiles at me. "I love you, Santos."

My nose scrunches. "What?"

"You're a good man. A great brother. You too, Cruz. I

wanted you here because... because..." She looks up at Salvador, and while I can tell Cruz knows what she's about to say, I still have no clue.

Salvador rests his hand on her shoulder. "I've asked Eva to marry me, and she's accepted."

Adelita gasps, raising her hand to her mouth. "Oh, Eva! That's wonderful!"

Cruz is frozen, while Santiago looks on the scene pleasantly, curiously observing everyone to see what a normal reaction looks like.

Eva holds her brother's stony gaze. I can see clearly how much she longs for his approval. Really, she'll do what she likes either way, but there is an insecurity that's hard to miss. "Say something, Cruz."

Cruz steps back until his butt hits the wall. The back of his head rests against the hard surface as his eyes focus on the ceiling. "This is what you want?"

"Yes. I love him."

Then Cruz levels his gaze on Salvador. "Is he worthy?"

Eva answers a quick, "Yes," in time with Salvador's swift, "No."

"Good answers," Cruz replies.

Cruz meets my eyes and then glances at Adelita, as if to ask me if we will marry Adelita someday.

I don't know the answer to that. All I know is that my family is growing larger, and with it, my heart.

Cruz's voice is stern. "You're leaving Cáceres?"

Eva's lips purse. "No, Cruz." Her fingers twine through Salvador's. I can tell they have talked this through as she gears up to deliver the rest of the news. "We'd be uniting the two tribes. Anzaldúa would come to live with us. We need protection, now that our army has been severely cut down. You know Salvador has been wanting to bring his people to the surface, now that Don Luis has passed on."

Eva trades a secretive look with Cruz that I don't understand. It's clear to me that something happened between Cruz and Salvador's father, Don Luis, but I don't care to dig to the bottom of it.

Cruz runs his hand over his face. "You ran this by Dad?"

Eva's eyes glisten. "He said he wants you to call him after I tell you." She hands Cruz her phone, but he's already pulled his device from his pocket. "I told him about our arrangement—that you don't want to rule the village. That you'd rather I took Dad's place when he hands down the ruling seat."

I hold in a breath, processing too much too fast. I was never under the impression that Cruz wanted to take his rightful ruling seat in Cáceres. Them telling this to Father José, however, makes it all real.

It's a good plan, really. Cruz doesn't know his own people well enough to lead them effectively. He would rather fight for their safety than sit through meetings about policy.

Eva is a natural leader. I have no doubt this is her destiny.

Cruz connects with Dad, and in the shortest conversation I've heard regarding the shift in a monarchy, Cruz confirms that no, he's never wanted the ruling spot. He's always been more comfortable on the front lines of a fight than to be the one making plans from afar. No matter their birth order, their personal choice should trump nature's suggestion.

Then Cruz puts Dad on speaker. "Eva, this is what you want?"

Eva's voice comes out choked. "Yes, Daddy."

There is too much silence. I want nothing more than good things for Eva. Cruz has never wanted to rule Cáceres.

But at the end of the day, this will be Father José's call.

The six of us wait without speaking or breathing while the future of Cáceres hangs in the balance.

19

A FATHER'S LOVE
ADELITA

*D*on José, Cruz, Eva and Salvador have been going back and forth for a good five minutes. I'm afraid to breathe too loudly; the situation is so fragile. Santos, Santiago and I are flies on the wall, listening to everything so we can see how a monarchy is run when communication is open and honest.

Don José is calm and methodical in his thinking, laying out one step at a time so the four of them can puzzle through it all together. "But the people need one voice, not two. If you are to marry Salvador, as you've told me you want to do, there will be confusion of if you are in charge or if it's Salvador."

I didn't think of this, but Salvador, apparently, has. He chimes in with a raspy, "Eva will lead. I will be her husband, helping her however she needs. Anzaldúa will follow her eventually, because they look to me. I will respect her rule, and Anzaldúa will fall in line."

Holy... My mouth falls open as I marvel at the man I once loathed. I didn't know that to merge the two tribes, one of the two leaders would have to cede their rule to the other. I mean, it makes sense, but it's information I didn't factor in.

Eva leans into Salvador's side, closing her eyes. I am moved right along with her. There isn't a touch of greed anywhere on Salvador. He truly does just want what's best for his people—even if that means he is not their leader.

There is a weighty silence, but when Don José finally speaks, I wonder why I ever doubted this great man's heart.

"Very well. I will prepare to put the merging of the two tribes into motion. I should like to sit down with both you and Salvador to hammer out all the details."

"Of course, Daddy."

Salvador replies with a gravelly, "Yes, Sir."

"Salvador should have a position of leadership under you, Eva. He has much to offer." Don José is all business, which is a side of him I rarely get to witness. "Eva, perhaps you and Salvador can be the ones to lead Anzaldúa to us when they're ready. Do you have a plan of how to fit the new civilians into Cáceres?"

Eva and Cruz lock eyes and then turn to me, silently begging me to push them through this big change.

This is their conversation, their tribe. I shouldn't be the one making decisions for Cáceres. Yet before I can stop myself, the cry of my heart spills into the air without regret. "Tear down the walls. Then we will have the room to expand and comfortably fit everyone."

Cruz closes his eyes, the corners of his mouth turning up at a slight angle. He shoos his sister from my side so he can take her place on the bed next to me. It's a narrow mattress, to be sure, but somehow we fit. He gathers me in his arms, resting his chin atop my head. I can feel contentment radiating off his body.

Santos tips a cup of water to my lips. When I take a few swallows, he massages my fingers, his eyes on the cell phone as if he wants to see his father's face during this very important conversation.

Salvador leans toward the phone. "Should you need help with the labor, Anzaldúa can lend a hand, if you can provide temporary lodging for the workers."

The second long pause is the one that gets my heart hammering.

Cruz jumps in. "Dad, the walls aren't who we are anymore. It can't be who we are if Cáceres is going to thrive and grow. It keeps out friends more than it keeps out enemies. That is not what Eva and I want."

Eva's chin lifts, holding tight to Salvador's hand.

Finally, Don José speaks. "No one in Cáceres is going to like this."

My heart falls. Doing what's right isn't often what's popular.

When Don José continues, I can hear the grin in his voice—perhaps in his very soul. "I love it. I've always wanted to go out to a scandal. This is good, kids. Your rule will start with something to mark it as yours. I admit, I never had the gall to attempt something so grand. I'm proud of you both."

Eva lets out a laugh that has a flood of tears mixed in, mingling her joy with a hint of hysteria. "Really?"

"Really. You are always the thing my heart needs, Eva."

I love when he says that. Gets me every time.

But Don José isn't done being wonderful. I doubt he'll ever stop being the parent we all need. "I'll help you, support you. We will make this happen. It's a good idea. And merging with Anzaldúa? You've added to our tribe, and you're giving me another son when you marry Salvador." Then, to Salvador, Dad says, "Salvador, welcome to the family. And welcome to Cáceres."

My heart swells to near bursting. I love this family. It's big and it's weird, but at the end of the day, there's nowhere I'd rather be than with these people who give beyond what anyone would expect.

Dad continues on without missing a beat. "I'll start Cáceres building new homes and expanding the territory to prepare for your arrival. Salvador, your extra men would be most appreciated. Six months' time should do it, if the population is as Salvador described." Then Dad pauses, and I can hear the love in his voice. "A year from your wedding, I will hand down the ruling spot to you, Eva."

Eva presses the back of her hand to her lips. "You will?"

"You have always put the people first. I don't want you to have to wait until I'm dead for you to take your rightful place. I want to be there to watch my daughter thrive."

Tears slide down Eva's cheeks. "Thank you, Daddy. I won't let you down."

"I love you, Eva. Salvador, Son, I'm glad you're a good man. Bring my daughters home safely."

"Absolutely, Sir."

"Dad. Call me Dad."

Salvador's eyes close and a tear slides down his cheek. I know the emotions that rise up in his chest, because they were mine when I was first taken in by this great man. We both needed a good dad, and we found the very best one.

Cruz ends the call, and all of us look around at each other in stunned silence. The wall is coming down. Cáceres is growing bigger. Another brother will be added to our family, and the first woman ruler in history will come from our tribe.

If there is a better ending for our story, I cannot imagine it.

Santos and Cruz squeeze my hands. I know that no matter what changes come our way, we will face them together.

EPILOGUE
CÁCERALDÚA

CRUZ

Adelita fidgeting with her dress makes me nervous. I worry that at any moment, she will realize this has all become too much. I mean, uniting Cáceres with Anzaldúa was one thing. It's been a year, and we're still adjusting, though not horribly. But Dad handing down his ruling spot to Eva? It's a lot for the village to get used to. Dad did well by Cáceres, but Eva is prepared to come into the position with fresh ideas and a whole new map of the place. Leave it to Eva to see the current expectation and raise it to the clouds.

My sister's wedding took place last year, but Eva still

looks like she just said "I do" to that clown. I still don't trust Salvador as far as I can throw him, but given that he's good to my sister and he's been nothing but an asset to Cáceres, I've decided to be less antagonistic about it all.

After I stole all his knives. Serves him right for not sharpening them. It's the only way he'll learn.

Santos is watching Adelita, too, and I can tell he's picked up on her fidgeting. There's not much that escapes his attention. Santos moves over to Adelita and leads her away from the crowd that's gathering on the other side of the long purple curtains that divide our family from Cáceraldúa.

That's what we've renamed our tribe, honoring both our great histories and acknowledging our promising future, now that we're joining together. Eva thought of the name, of course.

"I look weird," Adelita frets. "I don't need to be on the stage for this. It's only going to upset people. I wasn't born here."

Santos wraps Adelita's arms around his shoulders and takes his time kissing her, which is a surefire way to calm her down.

Why didn't I think of that?

Santos speaks slowly, lulling her with no trace of tension in his body. "Neither was I. Neither were half the people here. It's good that you and I are on the stage today. It will remind everyone that Father José values our blended heritages, and hopefully they will do the same." He nuzzles her nose. "No one has called me a savage in months. I think the merger is going well." He kisses her lips. "We belong here, *Corazón.*"

Santos is absolutely right, and I couldn't be prouder that he is the one saying it.

My sister bumps me as she walks by, so nervous that she doesn't even realize the mistake. "I stand where, now?" she asks Dad, who walks her through the ceremony once more. The platform in the Town Square will make us easily visible to everyone. When the curtains draw back, even though the two tribes have been living here together in peace for months now, today our merge will be official.

Cáceraldúa will be the name we rally around, and my sister will be their leader.

Eva looks regal, but that's nothing new. You could dress her in rags and she would still walk with her nose in the air, demanding the world behave as it should. She belongs in the golden dress she's got on now, with her hair braided in a crown.

I look like an idiot in my military threads. I can practically feel Rafi snickering at me from above. I shoot a scowl up to the sky, where the clouds haven't bothered us in months. Dad hasn't mentioned the inconvenience I used to cause the village with my moods being so attached to the weather as they are. But now that I've found a way to be less anxious, less upset, and... what did Aarón call it? Oh, right. Less ornery, the weather has evened out.

Santos sneaks Adelita to the side of the stage away from us, so he can kiss her without the family watching on wistfully. After Adelita finally got back on her feet earlier this year, the two of them haven't been able to keep a lid on their passion.

Santiago nudges my ribs. "Is my medal crooked? I can't get it right."

After joining the military, Santiago has been crucial in taking down the Kalku. While there are still factions out there, they've made it a point to hide from us, rather than attack. Santiago earned his first medal last month, and he's moved it from shirt to shirt, making sure to show it off everywhere he goes.

"Here. I'll fix it." I take out the pin and put it back in, somehow making it more crooked. "Uh, maybe I'm not the right person for the job. Santos is the one who puts mine in place."

Santiago frowns at the lopsided medal. "I don't want to interrupt them. I'll wait until he comes up for air."

"That might take a while."

Santiago chuckles and fiddles with his medal some more.

Tio Bruno comes to the side of the stage with Tavita on his arm. "Everyone ready?" he asks.

Tavita fusses with her hair. "I should be out there with the people, Bruno. There's no reason for me to be on the stage. I'll stand out."

Tio Bruno catches my eye out of the corner of his. "I think it's fine for me to have my fiancée by my side during a monumental day for Cáceraldúa."

My eyes widen. "Wait, what? Did I hear that right? Fiancée?" Sure enough, when I look down at Tavita's hand, a diamond ring sparkles on her finger.

"He asked me this morning," she says quietly, and then bats her hand at Tio Bruno. "I told you not to say anything! I wanted Adelita to know first."

Santiago grins at the two. "A wedding? Can I be the one who sets up the chairs for the ceremony? I did Eva's perfectly."

Santiago asks for the strangest things, but the odd tasks make him happy, so no one denies him a thing.

Tavita pinches the bridge of her nose. "Of course, Santiago."

Tio Bruno holds my gaze with a note of seriousness to him. "We were thinking of traveling for a while. Not sure how long. Hard to run the military when I'm on the road. You've been training the new soldiers. How do you think Salvador's men are doing?"

"They've still got a ways to go, but they're coming along. What help do you need while you're away?" I'm still catching up, unsure what people are supposed to do in this situation. Should I hug him? Congratulate him? Tell Tavita she could clearly do better than my surly uncle?

I cannot picture myself hugging my uncle. Even when I see him kissing Tavita, I'm often convinced it's an optical illusion.

Tio Bruno takes off the pin that marks him as our commander. I remember drawing a picture of the star and cutting it out so I could tape it to my shirt, pretending to be him when I was a little boy.

It happens so fast that I hardly register what he's done. "I think it's time for you to take over, Cruz. Tavita and I will be back when we feel like settling down, which might not be for a long time." When my mouth pops open, my uncle grips me by the nape of my neck, just like I do with Santos and Santiago when I need them to really hear that I love them. "It's your turn to protect the village. I trust you, Commander Cruz."

My heart hammers with uncertainty. It feels like I'm underwater, registering what's happened from a foggy distance. "You... I don't... Tio Bruno, you..."

He looks no less serious and no less intimidating than he always has, even as he takes a leap and draws me into his arms. He's unpracticed hugging men, but he makes the effort for me.

I thought this would be strange, but as it turns out, this was the one embrace I've gone my whole life needing.

Though I'm more muscular than he is now, I'm a little boy in his arms, trusting him to tell me I am capable of great things. Trusting that he knows me well enough to be sure when it's the right time to push me out into the world.

"I'm proud of you, Cruz," he whispers in my ear.

My whole body is tingling with newness, with surprise, and with wonder. I never dreamed he would say something so grand to me, but when he releases me, his eyes are wet, just like mine. "Thank you, Tio Bruno. I won't let you down."

"I know. You never have."

When Santos and Adelita join us, Santos gasps when he gets closer. "Tavita, is that... Are you...?" He points to her ring finger.

Tavita throws her head back. "I wanted to tell Adelita first! I'm terrible at this." She squares her shoulders to her sister. "Bruno asked me to marry him, and I said yes."

Adelita freezes, and then throws herself into her sister's arms, forgetting her nerves from before. "Oh, that's wonderful! You could do so much better, but I'm happy for you."

Tavita laughs loudly at the dig to Tio Bruno.

When Adelita pulls back, she turns to Tio Bruno with a serious face. "Okay, that means you're going to be my brother. I'd like a porch swing for the back of the house, and some cotton candy. I think any sister of yours deserves a puppy, too."

Tio Bruno glowers at her. I do not understand their relationship, but it amuses me every time they go at each other like this. "How about I settle for giving you an old knife and see how long it takes you to have a clumsy moment with it?"

"How about I get you a kitten for your wedding gift? Oh, I can see it now! That settles it. Don't register for a kitten; I'm getting you one."

He snarls at her. "I hate you so much."

This pleases Adelita for reasons I will never understand. "I love you too, Bruno. Now that you're my brother, I think you should go by Bunny-boo. It's perfect." She reaches up and pinches his cheek, adding to his scowl. "Welcome to the family, Bunny-boo."

"Can I throw her in the lake?" he asks Tavita.

"I'm afraid not, Beautiful. The ceremony is about to start."

Adelita kisses my cheek, but it's not enough. I lead her away from the others so we can have a semi-private moment before we're swept away by duty. When I show her my Commander's star, she grins at the new title. "You deserve it."

"It'll mean longer hours in the barracks," I remind her. "Santos will be my number two, though I haven't told him yet."

"I'm proud of you, Cruz. I've been working long hours in the clinic anyway. You're the right person for the job. This star looks good on you. And I always feel better if Santos is by your side."

I love that she's found her niche here in Cáceraldúa. No one balked when she opened up a therapy clinic. It was the perfect time, actually, what with all the change from the fallen soldiers and the merging of two villages. She takes on far too many patients, but it makes her come alive.

I think she's realizing the same about me when I am doing what I love.

Her hand slides up my bicep. "I really like the look of you in this uniform." Her voice is low, and I can tell that Santos didn't sate her desire, but merely got her riled up.

"I guess I'll let you strip it off me tonight, then."

I really love it when she's in my arms and ready for more.

"So much for life slowing down," she comments as she leans up on her toes to kiss me.

I can't help the chuckle that shakes my chest. "With you? I'm fairly certain the adventures will never stop coming."

Adelita kisses me again, and I know without a doubt that we will always find each other, no matter what storms life throws our way.

My father's voice booms over the crowd once the curtains part, gathering everyone and starting the ceremony.

Santos trots over to us, kissing Addy's cheek and then mine. "Let's get out there," he reminds us. "Eva will have our heads if we're not standing in the right spot."

The three of us make our way together—as it will always be—toward our family.

Toward our fate.

Toward our future.

The End

Love the series?
Please leave a review.

Thank you for joining me on this adventure.
I hope you enjoyed reading it as much as I loved writing it.

Hold my hand, dear reader.
We have many more worlds to explore together.

VENGEFUL PRINCE PREVIEW

Enjoy a free preview of "Vengeful Prince",
book one in the *Territorial Mates* series.

VENGEFUL PRINCE
GOING FOR A RUN

How a peace walk turned into running for my life, I'll never understand. This was a bad idea.

Even though I can see just fine through the night, the rain pelting my face makes the jutting rocks harder to detect. I've tripped three times already, and I just know it'll be an even four if I'm not careful. But there's not a spare second to invest in caution. The growl and snap of jaws close behind me light up a fear I know I'll never be able to outrun.

I don't know how Alex talked me into this, but if he ever suggests another hairbrained scheme, I'm saying no. I'm saying no so loudly that he actually hears me this time.

The smattering of trees thickens as I near the tall

border wall. The stone barrier I'm bolting toward in the distance is a clear message to all shifters that they don't want to travel through these woods.

They can't handle the lawlessness that lurks on the other side—which is exactly why I charge full-force toward it. Neutral Territory is for criminals and the outcasts of society. It's where shifters and vampires are forced to coexist, which is one of the most brilliant punishments our peoples can dream up.

The pursuing shifter's howl to rally his mates resounds through the night, so my legs pump harder as I breach the barrage of trees that usually warn people to stay away. Instead, I welcome them, knowing I'm not safe yet, but I'm on the edge of it. Most shifters won't do more than sniff near these woods, not even to snatch at a rogue vampire like me who's daft enough to traipse through enemy territory.

But I'm not their enemy. That was the whole point of the peace walk. To stroll through shifter territory and let them see we mean no harm. We're people, not blood-sucking monsters of the night.

Well, I mean, vampires do drink blood, and yes, we largely do our living during the night, but monsters? That's a bit of a reach.

The soft cadence of paws hitting leaves and

branches slows but doesn't stop completely, so I keep my swift pace. For a second, the sound stops, and everything in me brightens at the idea that I might get out of this with only a few bruises and a bloody nose.

When the canine shifter pummels me from behind, I realize he hadn't stopped, but jumped at me instead. His fangs sink into my shoulder as my chin hits the forest floor, my arm landing beneath my body with a sickening crunch. I roll onto my back the second he lets go, facing my assailant head-on. My forearm screams in agony, and I know something's too wrong to shake off.

Only slivers of moonlight shine through the twined branches overhead, glinting off my attacker's maw enough to highlight him backing up instead of lunging again. In a blink, he changes into his man form—a dark-haired brute with his hands raised in caution. "You're Prince Destino Karamathian? Why would ye... We wouldn't have..."

I stand, though that small feat takes more effort than I'm prepared for. "You wouldn't have attacked me if you knew you could be hanged for it? So it's alright to jump a vampire, so long as it's not me? Is that the sort of logic I'm hearing from you?"

He doesn't respond, which is probably best.

I wave him off. "Go back to your home and realize

that my biggest crime was walking. You bit me for *walking*. That's the sort of bloke you are. Be very proud you defended your territory from a pleasant stroll down the street. Brave soul, you are. Would you be able to sleep better at night if I bared my fangs to give you a good scare?"

"Not your fangs, your majesty!" the shifter pleads.

Oh, for clouds' sake. "Are you having a laugh? *You* bit *me!*"

He backs away, turns, and bolts out of the forest, leaving me alone in the woods. He's probably hoping I get too lost in here to find my way to report him. Little does he know I understand these woods better than he does, as well as the land that lies on the other side.

I was headed in that direction anyway, so I turn and trudge through what is rapidly becoming a muddy path, traveled usually only by my best friend. Salem's not going to be happy when he learns one of his own attacked me, but honestly, I'm not sure what Alex and Salem were expecting would happen. I can only hope they aren't as bad off as my arm feels.

Every bloody movement is an echo of pain through my forearm, shooting up my arm and zinging off the bite marks in my shoulder. It's a solid half a mile through the woods, and I take each step with care.

When the trees thin out to reveal the towering stone

wall that's meant to keep miscreants out of Jacoba, I shake my head at the flimsy logic of the shifters. "Like a wall could really keep us out if we wanted in," I say to the night.

Though, truly, this wall is far easier to scale without what I'm fairly certain is a broken arm. It's not impossible to climb, but I'm grateful I'm alone, so Salem and Alex don't see me sweat through the effort of making my way over the ten-foot-high stone barrier.

I stumble a few steps when my boots hit the earth on the other side, but manage to catch myself before I break any other limbs. The moonlight glints off the sharp, craggy boulders that welcome the unwelcomed to the outskirts of Neutral Territory.

I heave a sigh of relief that I'm nearly someplace safe. I could go home to the castle and let the healer give me a look, but then I'd have to report what happened. I don't want a shifter hanged on a vampire's order. I want peace.

Somehow.

The mountains are all black rock in this part of the land, and probably look formidable to anyone with a shred of sense. But to me, it looks like home, more than my own address.

I've many fond memories of practicing different styles of weaponry with Salem and Alex, talking politics, and trying to dream up a better future than the one that will be handed down to us. Our parents have made such a mess of things, that these angry-looking ebony rocks have been my safe place more times than I can count.

Though I never venture into the heart of Neutral Territory, I often travel on the outskirts and climb up to our cave overlooking the land of cast-outs. I wonder if they've lucked out and found the secret to happiness, living without the governing and often corrupt hand of the shifters, the vampires and the fae.

Though I'm not scheduled to meet here with Salem and Alex for a few hours, this is the place I'm called toward most often. It's quiet, and no one lies to me. No one hates me. No one dismisses me as useless because my ideas don't involve waging war on the shifter or fae territories.

So I climb. Even though I'm doing it one-handed, I move up the side of the mountain, working my way around the side so I can rest in our secret cave. It's far enough away from the damage that might always be unfixable.

This was a bad idea.

The rocks are bloody slippery from the intermittent rain. It's not pelting me at the moment, but judging by the clouds hovering over the mountaintop, it won't be long before I'm making my way up to our cave in the dark, in the rain, with a broken arm.

My fingers slip, and my heart jumps into my throat in time with my foot scrambling to find its hold. Despite my apparently "monstrous" ability to see in the dark, this mountain is still problematic when scaling it with one usable arm. I'm just grateful my mates aren't watching me struggle.

With a surge of desperation to get to level ground before my only functional arm gives out, I hoist myself up again and again, my forearm straining. My teeth grind as I grunt through the last few feet, finally glimpsing the ledge with a cry of relief.

I'm almost there. I won't fall. I won't fall.

My fingers slip, and a cry belts out from me. The sound scares me more than the few inches I slip before I manage to catch myself.

"Why, is that the great Prince Destino Karamathian?" Alex's voice hits my ears from two feet above my head.

A lantern's light flicks on and shines into the night to guide the way more clearly.

"It can't be," Alex continues, enjoying himself a bit too much. "Prince Destino doesn't climb like an elephant and sweat like a bride on her wedding night."

I glance up, and his face pops out from the cave's

mouth. His blond hair falls forward, framing the wry grin that greets me.

Alex's smile vanishes when he sees my struggle. "Des, what have you gotten yourself into this time?"

Binge the entire *Territorial Mates* series today!

ABOUT THE AUTHOR

USA Today bestselling author Mary E. Twomey lives in Michigan with her three adorable children. She enjoys reading, writing, vegetarian cooking, and telling her children fantastic stories about wombats.

While she loves writing fantasy, dystopian, and paranormal tales for her readers, Mary also writes romance under the name Tuesday Embers, and cozy mysteries under the name Molly Maple.

Visit her online at www.maryetwomey.com.
Sign up for her newsletter, so you never miss a new release.